Love on the Road 2015

First published in 2015 by
Liberties Press
140 Terenure Road North | Terenure | Dublin 6W
T: +353 (1) 405 5701|E: info@libertiespress.com | W: libertiespress.com

Trade enquiries to Gill & Macmillan Distribution
Hume Avenue | Park West | Dublin 12
T: +353 (1) 500 9534 | F: +353 (1) 500 9595 | E: sales@gillmacmillan.ie

Distributed in the United Kingdom by
Turnaround Publisher Services
Unit 3 | Olympia Trading Estate | Coburg Road | London N22 6TZ
T: +44 (0) 20 8829 3000 | E: orders@turnaround-uk.com

Distributed in the United States by
IPM | 22841 Quicksilver Dr | Dulles, VA 20166
T: +1 (703) 661-1586 | F: +1 (703) 661-1547 | E: ipmmail@presswarehouse.com

ISBN: 978-1-909718-58-6
2 4 6 8 10 9 7 5 3 1

A CIP record for this title is available from the British Library.

Cover design by Karen Vaughan – Liberties Press
Internal design by Liberties Press

The publishers gratefully acknowledge
financial assistance from the Arts Council.

Love on the Road 2015

Twelve More Tales
of Love and Travel

Edited by
Sam Tranum and Lois Kapila

```
LIB
ERT
IES
```

Table of Contents

Foreword

This anthology is the product of the Love on the Road writing contest, which we ran between May and July of 2014. In our call for submissions, we asked writers around the world to send us their tales of love and travel, true or imagined.

This is the second time we've run the contest. The first iteration, in 2013, resulted in the anthology *Love on the Road 2013: Twelve Tales of Love and Travel*. We enjoyed it so much that we decided to do it again.

This time around, writers sent stories to us from Australia, Belgium, Canada, Italy, India, Ireland, Malawi, New Zealand, the Philippines, the UAE, the UK and the US. We selected our favourite twelve stories, which are published in this anthology. Nod Ghosh's 'Janus: A Path to the Future' is true; the rest are fiction.

We then sent these twelve stories to our panel of judges, who selected the contest winners. First prize went to Shirley Fergenson for 'Not a Finger More'. Second prize went to Tendayi Bloom for 'Manila Envelope'. And third prize went to Marlene Olin for 'Sunrise Over Sausalito'.

We would like to thank the judges: Alexander Cochran, an agent with London's Conville & Walsh; Amanda Festa, managing editor of Boston's *Literary Traveler*; Lucas Hunt, director of New York's Orchard Literary; Jessu John, a Bangalore-based journalist and writer; and Vanessa

O'Loughlin, founder of Irish publishing consultancy The Inkwell Group.

Thanks also to all those who were kind enough to share their writing with us.

—Sam Tranum and Lois Kapila
Dublin, January 2015

About the Authors

Tendai Huchu, who wrote 'The Queue', is the author of *The Hairdresser of Harare*. His short fiction and nonfiction have appeared in *The Manchester Review*, *Ellery Queen's Mystery Magazine*, *Gutter*, *AfroSF*, *Wasafiri*, *Warscapes*, *The Africa Report*, *The Zimbabwean*, *Kwani?* and numerous other publications. His new novel, *The Maestro, the Magistrate and the Mathematician*, has just been released in Zimbabwe.

Marlene Olin, who wrote 'Sunrise Over Sausalito', has had stories published in *Upstreet Magazine*, *Vine Leaves*, the *Saturday Evening Post* online, *Emry's Journal*, *Biostories*, *Edge*, *Poetica*, *Arcadia*, *Ragazine*, *Poydras Review* and the *Jewish Literary Journal*. In the coming months, her work is forthcoming in *Meat for Tea*, *The Broken Plate* and *Escape Your World*, a collection distributed by Scribes Valley Publishing. Born in Brooklyn and raised in Miami, Marlene attended the University of Michigan. She lives in Coconut Grove, Florida with her husband. She has two children and two grandchildren. She recently completed her first novel.

Shirley Fergenson, who wrote 'Not a Finger More', was raised in Harrisburg, Pennsylvania. She received her undergraduate degree cum laude from the University of Pittsburgh in 1973, having majored in English. Shirley moved to Baltimore, Maryland in 1974. After raising four children, she returned to university and received an MA in fiction writing from Johns Hopkins University in 2005. Shirley has continued to reside in Baltimore, with some time spent in Costa Rica and Santa Fe, New Mexico. Since 2001, she has served as the literary fiction specialist at The Ivy Bookshop, an independent bookseller in Baltimore. Her fiction has been published in the *Baltimore Review*.

Nod Ghosh, who wrote 'Janus: A Path to the Future', lives in Christchurch, New Zealand, where she has completed a creative writing course at the Hagley Writers' Institute. Her short stories and poems have been published by *Takahe*, *Christchurch Press*, *Flash Frontier*, *TheGayUK* and *Penduline Press*. She has won several writing prizes and competitions. Nod is currently writing her second novel, *The Iris Tattoo*. Many years ago, an aunt urged Nod to take up writing. On thanking the aunt for her perceptive insight, she was told, 'Oh, it wasn't to do with the way you write. You were born on the 23 April, such an auspicious date, the Bard's birthday. I felt you ought to be a writer too.'

Ghosh titled her story 'Janus: A Path to the Future' because, in Roman mythology, Janus was the god of beginnings and transitions. Often depicted as having two faces, he watched over doorways, gates and passages. Looking in both directions, Janus oversaw the future and the past.

Catherine McNamara, who wrote 'Enfolded', grew up in Sydney and studied visual communication and African and Asian modern history before moving to Paris. She worked in pre-war Mogadishu and lived for ten years in Accra, where she co-managed a bar and art gallery. She now lives in Italy, where her jobs have included translating welding manuals, physics papers and World War I signage in the Dolomites. She plays classical piano, loves telemark skiing and has impressive collections of African sculpture and Italian heels.

McNamara's collection *Pelt and Other Stories* was longlisted for the Frank O'Connor Prize 2014 and a semi-finalist in the Hudson Prize in 2011. Her stories have been shortlisted and published in anthologies by Virago, the University of Plymouth and Labello Press. Her story 'Magaly Park' (Labello Press) received a Pushcart Nomination in 2014, and 'The Wild Beasts of the Earth Will Adore Him' was shortlisted in the inaugural Hilary Mantel/Kingston University Short Story Prize. She has also published an erotic comedy, *The Divorced Lady's Companion to Living in Italy* (Indigo Dreams Publishing UK) and a children's book, *Nii Kwei's Day* (Frances Lincoln Publishing).

Stanley Kenani, who wrote 'We Will Dance in Lampedusa', is a Malawian writer, one of the winners of the SA PEN/HSBC Literary Award. He was short-listed for the Caine Prize for African Writing in 2008 and 2012. In August 2011, Random House Struik in South Africa published his first book, *For Honour*, a collection of eleven short stories which present the nation of Malawi as a theatre of the absurd, where minority groups such as gays and lesbians are oppressed, people struggle with issues such as childlessness, and major problems like marital rape and human trafficking are suffered in silence. Stanley is working on his first full-length novel.

Barry Reddin, who wrote 'At the Mouth of the River', is an Irish writer and theatre director currently living and working Brussels. Originally from Portlaoise, Ireland, Bar studied fine art at the Waterford Institute of Technology before relocating to Belgium where he is teaching at the English Youth Theatre in the European capital.

Tendayi Bloom, who wrote 'Manila Envelope', is a migration-policy researcher currently based in Barcelona, Spain. It was while in Manila in the Philippines for work in 2012 that she got the idea for her story. Tendayi's published fiction appears in the anthologies *She's The One: Anyone Can Be a Heroine* (2013) and *Ferry Tales* (2013) and she is now finishing her first short-story collection, set in Whitechapel, in the East End of London. Her fiction is influenced by her academic and policy work on migration and noncitizen justice, which can be found in reports, journals and blog posts. She also tweets on these themes @TendayiB

Lily Mabura, who wrote 'Kaveh Mirzaee and the Woman from Lashar', is an assistant professor of English at the American University of Sharjah, in the UAE. She has a PhD in English from the University of Missouri-Columbia, in the USA. She was a pre-doctoral dissertation fellow at the Frederick Douglass Institute for African and African-American Studies, University of Rochester, New York. Her areas of research and teaching include women's studies, gender studies, post-colonial studies and creative writing. Her first collection of stories is titled *How Shall We Kill the Bishop and Other Stories* (African Writers Series, Heinemann-Pearson, 2012). Her fiction awards include the

Ellen Meloy Fund for Desert Writers Award, the Jomo Kenyatta Prize for Literature, and the National Book Week Literary Award – Kenya. Mabura has also published a novel and several children's books.

Jackie Davis Martin, who wrote 'In the Heat', divides her life (so far) into thirds: childhood in Pennsylvania, parenthood in New Jersey, maturation, of sort, in California. Her vocation of teaching literature has consistently blurred into the avocation of reading and writing. She's taught high school in English on both coasts and presently teaches at City College in San Francisco, a city where she and her husband pursue – almost relentlessly – the plethora of arts and scenery that San Francisco and the Bay Area offer.

She has had stories and essays published in journals that include *Flash, Flashquake, Fastforward, JAAM, 34th Paralell* and *Sleet*. Her most recent work is in *Bluestem, Enhance, Counterexample Poetics, Fractured West, Dogzplot* and *Gravel*. Her novella *Extracurricular*, was a finalist in the Press 53 Awards of 2011, and a short piece won second place in *Past Loves Competition and Journal*. Several stories have been anthologised, most recently in *Modern Shorts* and *Love Is a Rollercoaster*. A memoir *Surviving Susan*, which deals with the death of her daughter, was published in 2013. Jackie is presently working on a short story collection.

Alice Bingner, who wrote 'Honeymoon in Mata de Limon', was raised in the village of Lapeer, Michigan, in the USA. As an adult, she has chosen to reside in small and remote places. She spent three fascinating years in Grand Cayman and six months in Grand Turk, before these islands became well-known, as well as five years in a railroad village called Mata de Limón, in Costa Rica. She lived in Texas for two years and Florida for eight, as well as in California and Mexico. She now permanently resides in Ann Arbor, Michigan. Each of her four children has at times shared her exotic adventures.

Journalism was her career of choice – reporting, editing, proofreading and feature writing on weeklies, a daily, a monthly newspaper and a monthly magazine. Rivalling her fascination with writing has been her interest in teaching English as a second language, first as a volunteer for six months in Tapachula, Chiapas, Mexico and then for two years at Bridge International School in Florida.

Now retired, she has written *The Cayman Islands as They Crest: Letters to Eunie*, about her first year in those islands. She is contemplating another that will incorporate Mata de Limón, her unique 1972 discovery.

Gregory J. Wolos, who wrote 'Refugees of the Meximo Invasion', lives and writes in upstate New York, on the bank of the Mohawk River. His short fiction has recently appeared or is forthcoming in *Post Road*, *Silk Road Review*, *Nashville Review*, *A-Minor Magazine*, *JMWW*, *Yemassee*, *The Baltimore Review*, *The Madison Review*, *The Los Angeles Review*, *PANK*, *A cappella Zoo*, *Superstition Review* and many other print and online journals and anthologies. His stories have earned four Pushcart Prize, Best of the Small Presses nominations, and his latest collection was named a finalist for the 2012 Flannery O'Connor Short Fiction Award. For a full list of his publications and commendations, visit www.gregorywolos.com.

1.
The Queue
Tendai Huchu

Tinotenda arrived just after ten in the morning and took his place in line. He knew right away that going on a bender the previous night had been a big mistake. The month end used to be fun. Back in the day, when he did his training, they used to look forward to their monthly cheques. There were fewer zeroes then – hell, he wasn't even a millionaire – but you got more bang for your buck. His head throbbed and he promised God he would never drink that evil Eagle beer again. All God had to do in return was resume supplies of Castle, or even Lion. Was that too much to ask for? The Israelites got manna, Zimbabweans only wanted beer.

'Is this the one for the post office?' he asked the fat man in the Hawaiian shirt in front of him. The blue waves, tropical palms and surfboards were rather curious in a landlocked country.

'I stood in that one for thirty minutes before I realised it was for bread!' the fat man replied. A whiff of bad breath hit Tinotenda.

'So this one is for the post office?'
'What do you think?'
'If I knew I wouldn't be asking you.'

Tinotenda massaged his temples. The fat man turned away in a huff. What was that about? Tinotenda wondered. He studied the cool, hypnotic waves of the shirt and considered whether it was prudent to ask the next man in the queue. It would take some manoeuvring to get around the heap of Hawaiian flesh. A hand tapped his shoulder.

'*Bhudi*, is this the queue for the post office?' a small woman in a georgette dress asked him.

'I don't know,' he replied honestly. 'It should be. I certainly hope it is.'

The woman raised her eyebrows but she did not say anything. It was not uncommon for people to jump into a queue first and ask questions later. The mid-morning sun pulsed down on them. The tar shimmered under the sun's oppressive brilliance, creating a mirage like cool water flowing down a stream. There wasn't a cloud in the sky. A prison lorry ambled along slowly on its way to the magistrates' court. The prisoners were all dressed in white. Their shaved heads glistened and they became a throng of brown mirrors, dazzling and brilliant. The guards stood at the front, FN rifles resting casually at their sides. The lorry jolted as it hit a pothole and rolled on.

'Hold my place. I will go up front and ask someone,' the woman said.

He watched her walk past the fat man, studying her bony frame, swaying hips, elegant gait. The fat man was watching too, nodding his head appreciatively. A man dressed in blue overalls joined the queue and Tinotenda told him there was a woman before him. The man wanted to know if this was the queue for the post office. He would have to wait for the woman. The boutique to their left was almost bare. Still, it was open, selling pirated cassettes. *Sungura* music blared out, distorted by damaged speakers. It was shrill, with a hiss behind the wailing, depressed electric guitar. The song was a popular one:

> Oweoo oweoo oweoo
> My brother died
> My wife left me
> My son is a cripple
> I have no other children
> My father and mother are dead
> Now I am dying.
> Who will bury me?
> Oweoo oweoo oweoo

And so it goes. Tinotenda fought the pangs from his empty stomach, the feeling of bile rising. The woman returned and took her place in the queue.

'You're a teacher aren't you?' she asked with a smile.

'Are we in the right queue?'

'I noticed the chalk dust on your trousers.'

The man in the overalls was craning forward to hear. She held vital information and was keeping everyone waiting. There was an air of suspense. Others, who'd since joined the queue, also waited on her verdict – right queue or nay. Tinotenda reasoned that she wouldn't have been in this position of power if the fat man hadn't been a jackass. This was the Information Age, after all.

'Yes, I am a teacher. Now please answer my question: a) yes, b) no.'

'Which school?' she asked.

'Oh, for the love of Jesus who died for all our sins!' the man in overalls cried out.

'Okay, I'm just joking, this is the right queue,' she said, a smirk on her face.

There was a collective sigh of relief from the crowd that was growing behind them. They moved three steps forward and stopped again. A small victory against crushing inertia was won in that movement. It was progress. Tinotenda recalled a slogan he taught his pupils: forward ever, backward never.

He thought of changing banks. The Post Office and Savings Bank had been his bank since childhood, but it seemed the service only became slower and worse with the years. He'd stuck with them through the '90s when the government had floated a bizarre proposal to raid savers' deposits to fund war veterans' annuities. They'd decided against that in the end. It was easier just to print the money. Tinotenda felt he would be better off with Standard Chartered, Barclays or even CABS. There were queues in those other banks, yes, but they seemed to move faster. The folks who stood in those queues, as a rule, were better dressed, to the extent of even wearing purposeful looks.

The man in overalls verbally calculated whether he could make the bread queue next. A woman behind him said he would have been better off bringing someone else with him so they could have got places in both queues. She went on to explain that that's what she'd done, and that she also had a child in the bottle-deposits queue at TM. There was a hint of pride in her voice, as if holding places in three queues simultaneously was a triumph in itself.

I wish I'd got a post in Harare, Tinotenda thought. He

hated Bindura, its smallness, the old colonial buildings, the slow pace of life, how everyone knew one another. The street-lights seldom worked. ZESA hammered the town with load-shedding but mysteriously maintained power to the mines. That was all there was to the town: a huge gold mine and an even bigger nickel mine. The men in overalls and khakis strutted about the place like they owned it and thumbed their noses at people like him. To them, it seemed being unem-ployed was a lot more respectable than being a pen-pusher. The little town had one main road that you could walk down, from end to end, in less than a quarter of an hour. Tinotenda wondered how he'd ended up in such a backwater dump.

'I'm a student you know,' the woman in the georgette said.

He bowed his head slowly. Even the slightest movement made his brain feel like it was banging against his skull. He was assaulted by Hawaiian blue in front of him, and her dazzling orangey autumn colours from behind.

'Have you got any Cafemol?' he asked.

She rummaged through her denim handbag and handed him a pack of Anadin.

'Thanks,' he said, taking two and handing the pack back.

The queue inched forward, one more small victory – two, if he counted the tablets. That was the only way to take things these days. It was easy to get caught up in a spiral of despair. The woman was looking at him intently, as if wait-ing for him to say something else.

'What are you studying?' he asked.

'I'll give you two guesses.'

'Look, I'm grateful for the pills, but I'm not really in the mood.'

'Your eyes are very red.'

She turned away from him and looked down the road to the GG Café, door wide open, shelves empty. Why did they bother opening up? Why did they keep coming to work? Why didn't everyone just curl up and die quietly? Tinotenda wondered what it was that kept the entire nation going. He saw news reports of starving folk in the rural areas. They reminded him of pictures from Somalia in the early 90s, when he was still at college. In the face of this never-ending misery, there was something, hidden – an elementary particle, fundamental, unknown to science – that said life was still worth clinging on to. The worse things became, the more precious it seemed.

'We must be mad,' he said to no one in particular.

'Depends on how you define madness,' the woman said to him.

'What's your name?'

'Sithabile – Star, to you.'

'How can you be so cheerful in this?' He gestured, his hand making a wide sweep across the bleak street. *Oweoo oweoo oweoo.*

'How can I not be, Mr Teacher? What people don't understand is the true meaning of queues. They think queues are an inconvenience. A waste of time. But are they? Think of where we would be right now if there was no queue. We'd all be in the post office, scrambling, punching, scratching – survival of the fittest. No, queues are the height of civilisation. The last line of defence against chaos.'

'It's this passivity that got us into this situation in the first place.' Tinotenda watched the fat man let a friend cut in front of him, forcing everyone to take a step back. 'You see what I'm talking about?'

'The alternative is so much worse. You forget that at the end of the queue lies hope. That's what is in your heart right now. The faith that your fellow men will keep their places, despite all provocation, and that at the end of it we will all attain our goal. The queue forces us to put trust in our fellow man.'

'What are you studying?'

'Marketing, at the Bindura University.'

'One day you will be selling positions in queues at the rate you're going.'

'I'll be selling hope,' she said with a smile, as if she were the teacher, full of infinite patience, speaking to a pupil who just didn't get it.

An old woman walked by with a reed basket on her head. Tinotenda stopped her and bought two freezits for a few grand. He gave one to Star. She looked surprised and thanked him. He sucked the cold juice and downed his Anadin. Litter tumbled down the road, blown by a gentle wind which mercifully cooled them. Maize cobs, plastic bottles, paper bags, leaves and debris floated by, dancing in the wind as they went.

Cars were lining up on the lane opposite. They were aimed at the Total garage at the T-junction ahead. A tanker had just arrived and was pumping fuel into the tank. The drivers waited patiently, their engines switched off to save precious fuel. A few were on their cell phones, no doubt telling friends there'd been a petrol delivery. A pickup going in the opposite direction spotted this queue, made an abrupt U-turn and joined in. Tinotenda listened to the hum of the tanker. He watched the garage attendants in the shade, chatting with the tanker driver as they watched their new queue grow longer and longer.

The post office was coming into view now. It was a small, cream-coloured colonial building with a red-tiled roof. Standing in the middle of the town, it flew a multi-coloured Zimbabwean flag alongside a blue one for the postal service. The flags fluttered in the wind. To Tinotenda's dismay, a guard in green overalls and a green hard hat stepped out.

'It's lunch hour,' the guard announced.

He used his baton to separate those who were inside from those at the entrance and shut the doors.

'Unbelievable,' said Tinotenda.

'Well, they have to eat something too, don't they?' Star said.

'I'm not saying they shouldn't have a break. But wouldn't it make more sense for them to stagger their breaks so service isn't disrupted?'

'Isn't it better for them to eat together, like a family?' Star was unconcerned. It was as if she hadn't a care in the world. Tinotenda decided she was young and she hadn't seen a world before this one. This abnormality was her version of normal, and so she accepted it.

'What are we going to do with our lunch hour?' He couldn't mask the sarcasm in his voice.

Tinotenda sat down on the pavement. He leant his back against the wrought-iron burglar bars of Sales House. He turned and saw a few outfits inside, and staff looking forlornly outside. He used to shop in there, back in the day. He had an account at Edgars too. When did he last buy new clothes? Thank goodness for the flea market, with its bales of used American clothes, donated, now on sale.

Across the road, he watched the queue of vehicles move forward – making progress. He'd long since stopped dreaming of ever owning a car. He was pushing thirty, around that age one begins to make peace with the world, worn down by years of compromise and dreams that have turned to nought. It was now clear to him that a roof over his head and at least one square meal a day was all he could ever ask for. A pickup with a Trojan Horse, the mine's logo, was bumper to bumper with a blue Toyota Cressida. The driver of the pickup was his age, square-jawed and confident.

The Anadins were kicking in. The headache eased off. The sun had drifted overhead, so they were now in the shade of the shop verandas. Flakes of peeling paint rained down like snow from the asbestos roofing sheets. *Oweoo oweoo oweoo.* An old Peugeot 405 coughed up acrid black smoke as it inched forward. Beads of sweat formed on Tinotenda's face. He took slow breaths and waited. It reminded him of the last election. He'd queued all day to vote. Within a week he had learnt that his vote had not counted. It had changed nothing. Every time he was in a queue, he could not help thinking that the whole country was waiting, waiting for something. But each queue only led to the next and the next and the next – an infinity of queues stretching out through space and time.

They heard the old doors of the post office creak open. Slowly, they stood and faced forward once more. The feeling that he was making progress returned as they shuffled a few steps forward. Tinotenda tried to gauge the distance to the doors against the speed they'd been moving at and calculated that he was going to make it. A woman walked by carrying a bundle of firewood on her head. With one hand, she cradled a baby, who suckled on her left breast, which was poking out through her torn blouse. With the other, she carried a gallon of cooking oil. People walked to and fro. The town was always packed at the end of the month.

'What do you want to do when you finish uni?' he asked Star.

'Anything, the world is my oyster.'

'You're kidding right?'

'Why should I be? There are opportunities here. Most people just don't see them because they're locked up in their self-pity. I mean look at us right now. All these people in a queue to get money. If I stood in front of the post office with the right product, I'd take all their money away in a heartbeat.'

'You could sell a fridge to an Eskimo.'

'Or maybe to a Shona,' she laughed.

He noticed her pearly white teeth and the flawless caramel skin that glistened with a sprinkling of sweat on her brow. Her eyes were hazel and twinkled when she smiled. Tinotenda was lost, hypnotised in them, until he realised he was being rude, staring. He abruptly turned away, feeling embarrassed. He could feel his heartbeat. One, two, one, two.

They inched forward, making progress. Time slowed down in the queue as the burning sun arced through the sky. His thoughts drifted from his landlord to Star and back to his landlord. The rent was going up again; his salary was not. Star, Star, Star, twinkling behind him. *Teachers and students – oil and water*, he thought.

There were so many voices in the queue, talking at once. People who had been strangers just hours earlier now discovered some bond. Some spoke about the rains, which had failed to fall again. A voice, right at the back, was loudly revealing how it had noticed a pattern and come up with a foolproof strategy for winning the lotto. Someone asked for the method, but the voice refused, choosing instead to talk about how it was going to spend the money.

'Jesus has done miracles for me this year. He can do miracles for you too,' a woman at the front with a shrill voice was saying.

'No, no, no . . . it's not a pyramid scheme, it's called multi-level marketing. You pay five million, then you can go for meetings in Harare. When you get ten people to join, and they get another ten to join, you are given fifty million. My cousin who made me join has just harvested his fifty,' the fat man said to his queue-jumping comrade.

Tinotenda listened to the voices, his mind tripping, returning to Star, oscillating between her and the world around them. *We are the fish and the people are the sea.* The queue kept moving forward. Tinotenda smiled to himself as if there were no one else about. He now stood at the threshold.

The guard emerged and held his baton to Tinotenda's chest. It was a short, stout phallus with a rope that was tied around the guard's wrist.

'Right, there is no more money. It is finished,' he said.

'We've been here all day!' the overalls man shouted.

'We don't print money here. Come back tomorrow. There's nothing I can do. Don't shoot the messenger.'

The guard bolted the door, locking them out.

Tinotenda saw how close he was. Had the fat man's friend not jumped the queue, he'd have made it. The people in the queue hung about for a while, as though they expected the guard to come out and say it was a prank. A few voices of dissent grumbled for form's sake and then fizzled out. Tinotenda felt a hand on his shoulder.

'I guess we'll meet here tomorrow, same time?' Star said.

'A little earlier may be better.'

He watched her walk away until she was swallowed up by

the crowd. She was autumn orange, appearing and disappearing, twinkling, twinkling as she went. Tinotenda walked away a happy man; he had a date tomorrow with the queue.

2.
Sunrise over Sausalito
Marlene Olin

Monroe Rosenberg figured that a nursing home was like a hotel. He had checked himself into the South Beach Senior Center. By God he could check himself out.

His downward slide began the day he hit eighty. He ate lunch at the Van Dyke, bought himself a *New York Times*, and was taking his usual three-mile stroll up and down the Lincoln Road Mall. Suddenly, a crack in the pavement appeared out of nowhere. He lurched forward and landed like a tumbled bag of groceries. His eyeglasses flew in one direction, his cane another. A tropical breeze blew his newspapers like tumbleweeds along the street.

Monroe had prided himself on both his independence and his good health. When his wife Goldie died ten years earlier, he didn't cry in his soup like other widowers. He learned which buttons to push on the microwave and how to wash his clothes. Monroe had served four years in the Navy unscathed. Now a simple flaw in the cement redirected his life. His hip cracked like an egg.

The visions started the first week in the rehab centre. Monroe was wide awake. He tackled Sudoku puzzles and kept track of his investments. There was nothing wrong with his mind. And keeping your thoughts intact was no easy task in an institution. Half of the patients spoke Spanish while the other half spoke to Elvis. So when the visions flashed on his TV screen, right there in Technicolor like a commercial, he didn't flinch.

One minute he was watching CNN and the next minute he was watching his funeral. A rabbi he didn't recognise stood at a podium. As old and stooped as Monroe, his liver-spotted hands grew shakier from one vision to the next. For the next seventeen minutes, the rabbi would tell a story so distorted and distanced from the truth that it was only at the end that Monroe realised it was about him.

'And now will you please bow your heads and say a prayer for our friend and neighbour, not to mention beloved uncle, Monroe Rosenberg.'

Then the crowd – the men straight from the golf course in their pastel-coloured shirts, a handful of Goldie's friends in pearls and going-to-synagogue suits – chanted Kaddish. In the front row sat Goldie's nephew Carter. Curling his fingers into a fist and thwacking his chest, he out-cried them all.

For years, Carter had been like a son. He had been directionless, bouncing from one job to the next. Then one night Goldie sat Monroe down at their kitchen table. She had baked *mandlebreit* and made him tea. Monroe dunked the cookie into the cup, counted the seconds, extracted the cookie and, just as he was taking that first satisfying bite, Goldie launched a surprise attack.

'My nephew Carter, I know he's been a *schlimazel*, a constant source of worry to my poor sister, but he tries hard. What he needs is a break. An opportunity. I was thinking maybe at the Woodmere store, you could show him the ropes.'

Monroe had a gift for business. First one clothing store than another had sprung up like mushrooms, all over Long Island. Monroe admitted he could use the help. Soon, he and Carter were visiting the factories in China, hefting bolts of fabric, checking dye lots, inspecting samples for defects and pulls. Then, a year before Goldie's death, just when they figured out the chemo wasn't working, Carter stole Monroe's list of contacts. By the time they called in the hospice people, Carter had opened his own chain.

Monroe had never known such betrayal. And now Carter sat in the first row like the heir apparent, commandeering the high-profile seats with his third or fourth wife – who could keep track? – and blowing his nose like a bugle.

'Did you see that?' Monroe pointed to the TV. It wasn't one of those fancy models that hung on the wall. This one was a behemoth, an antique, a box thirty-six inches wide, plopped on a black plastic cart.

'Wardell, I'm talking to you. Are you deaf?'

The black orderly looked around, hoping there was someone else in the room. He stared at his reflection in the mirror. Green scrubs, latex gloves, his bald head in need of a fresh shave.

'You want me to change the channel?'

Monroe felt like a prisoner in his own body, caged by bed rails one minute, tethered to his wheelchair the next.

'Look. Look at that for Christ's sake! The man with the hat is the rabbi. That idiot in the first row is my nephew Carter. Don't you see them? Don't you see them?'

The orderly walked over to Monroe's hospital bed, plumped the pillows, sighed.

'Mr R, you seem a bit agitated.'

'A washing machine gets agitated. This is not agitated.' His cheeks blotched purplish red, Monroe began to shout. 'Do I look agitated?'

Up and down the rows, Monroe searched for faces from his past. He had been an only child. His father had been a haberdasher in Brooklyn, his mother a seamstress. They worked with their hands while the radio blared, their lives in rhythm with their machines.

They called him a change-of-life baby – a baby that comes after you've converted the empty nursery into a sewing room. They were going to move out West, they always told Monroe, but his birth changed everything. His mother, a blond, blue-eyed beauty, had dreamt of travelling the world. She framed magazine pictures of California and hung them up on walls of their home. The Golden Gate Bridge. Yosemite. Lake Tahoe. Whenever she'd walk by them, she'd touch them with her fingertips as if each were a *mezuzah* containing a hidden prayer. 'Life,' she would tell her son, 'sends you detours.'

Wardell shook his head. 'You should consider some of them pills, Mr R.'

'You can take my pills and shove them up your ass, Wardell. I hate pills! And they can't force me to take them either!'

There are a lot of crazy white people in here, but not this old man, thought Wardell. *This old man has all his pistons firing.* He smiled, unzipping his mouth slowly from one side to the other so that the old man could count his teeth.

'I imagine it's a gift, Mr R. Being a guest at your own funeral. It's a gift.'

Monroe raised his eyebrows. 'A gift?' The old man pointed a gnarled and crooked finger at the TV. 'This isn't a dream. It's more like a nightmare. And it's real, I tell you. As real as you are, standing in this room.'

Monroe lay back in his bed and rested his head. The orderly gently placed two fingers on his wrist and checked his pulse.

'I used to dream about my college graduation,' said the orderly. 'The dream seemed so real I could touch it. Like it was in fucking 3D. I was wearing that hat with the tassels, the long black gown, walking down the aisle. And there was my mama in the first row, crying and yelling my name. "Wardell! Wardell!" Sometimes the mind gets night and day confused. Hope and reality can get confused, too.'

The orderly had an accent, a Caribbean lilt to his voice. Up and down like ocean waves, the sounds began to lull Monroe to sleep. His eyelids fluttered. A shiver jolted his hand.

'Did you graduate?'

'Had to drop out the first semester. My father died. Never had a chance to go back.'

Whenever Monroe tried to remember his father, he couldn't visualise his face or hear his voice. Only a heavy brown coat came to mind. Monroe would be in his pyjamas, listening with his mother to Molly Goldberg, when his father would open the front door and let the wind rush in. Then he'd throw his tan fedora on their hall tree, take off his coat, and hang it in the closet. Monroe remembered a cuff, a sleeve. His father would be dead by the time he was five. Cancer. The chemicals in the hat factory, his mother would say. To this day, whenever a draft chilled the room, Monroe would picture that sleeve.

His uncle Hymie filled the gaps. If his mother was short with a mortgage payment, her brother would send a cheque. When Monroe got a girl in trouble, Uncle Hymie made those arrangements, too. All those years he and Goldie tried to get pregnant and nothing happened. But when he had been only sixteen, his chest still as hairless as a child's, he had knocked someone up. His uncle's receptionist no less.

For a short six months, he had been in love. Monroe was always a sturdy kid, built like a tree stump. Short, wide, grounded. When his uncle offered him a job at his furniture store, he couldn't turn down the extra cash. Bureaus, beds, tables. There was nothing Monroe couldn't lift. Soon he developed muscles he never knew existed. Bulges grew under his shirts.

Gretchen noticed. She was in her twenties. Her face and neck were talcum-powdered, her nails and her lips painted a bright fire-engine red. No girl, let alone a full-bodied woman, had ever taken an interest in Monroe before. Soon she was lurking in the supply closet and bumping into him in the halls. For a few short seconds the world spun.

When she told him she was pregnant, he couldn't believe a momentary blip – her hand on his zipper, his hand on her breast – was all it took. Monroe was sure he'd lose his job. He dreamt at night about the Bowery, living in a one-room tenement with Gretchen, the baby screaming all day and all night. But his uncle surprised him. Another detour, thought Monroe. Another path in a whole new direction.

'You know you're not the only fella in this woman's purview,' said Hymie. 'By God she has a black book! A black book with names!'

Monroe had been wondering why his uncle had hired a receptionist who couldn't type. Gretchen had a voice that squeaked like a rusty hinge. Customers hung up the phone when she answered.

'And every other month she threatens to show the god-damned book to your Aunt Myra!'

Maybe Hymie didn't want competition in the bedroom. Weeks later, he farmed Monroe out to another business-man. Carl 'Fits Like a Glove' Yankowitz. He sold women's shoes and accessories, whatever overstocks he could find. Monroe learned the retail-clothing business, and Hymie and Myra stayed happily married for almost fifty years. Friday nights, Monroe's mother would cook them dinner, her small way of saying thanks. Hymie, his breath soured from cigarettes, his big belly tugging at the buttons on his shirt, would sidle up to Monroe at the kitchen table.

'My friend Yankowitz, is he treating you right?'

Monroe knew Carl was cooking the books. He under-paid his help and *schtupped* the secretaries. 'He's treating me okay.'

'He's a *goniff*. A thief and a scoundrel. You couldn't pay for a better education!'

Hymie saw Monroe off when he boarded his first ship out to sea and stood alongside his mother at his wedding. Hymie lived long enough to meet Goldie. He liked Goldie. He always wanted them to have children right off the bat.

Carter wasn't the only fixture in his dreams. There was Abe Bernstein, who cheated at golf, moving the ball when he thought no one was looking. The stockbroker, he forgot his name, who always advised him to buy high and sell low. And Goldie's friends. Yetta or Etta. Marlene or Eileen. He wasn't sure. There they sat with their dyed black hair, dab-bing their orange cheeks with their tissues, looking in their compacts every five minutes to make sure their mascara hadn't run. God, how he hated those women. They surrounded Goldie like a tidal pool, circling her, feeding off of her good nature – *My, my we'd love an invitation to your country club!* – then abandoned her when she got sick. A get-well card, a potted plant, the detritus of friendship. Of all the villains who inhabited his visions, they were the worst.

Two months later, they moved Monroe from rehab into the nursing-home wing. Wardell got himself transferred, too. The two of them found a connection, a symbiotic relationship. They read the *New York Times* together, ogled *Baywatch* reruns on TV, and figured out ways to undermine the system. Monroe would fake symptoms and Wardell would pocket the drugs.

'*Symbiotic.* Write that down, Wardell.' Monroe had lifted another writing pad ('Lipitor: Don't Kid Yourself') from the nurses' station.

It was clear to him that the orderly was one of the more intelligent employees of the nursing home. Wardell was kind to the *alter kockers* reduced to bibs and diapers. He followed sports. He was reasonably well-informed about current events. Yet he had the vocabulary of an eight-year-old.

'We have a remunerative kinship, my friend. Write that down. *Remunerative.* I keep my head clear of medication and you keep yourself stocked in crack or meth or whatever else strikes your fancy.'

'I'm not an addict, Mr R. I told you. I ain't making money off your pills. They're more like barter. I'm using them to barter for things I need.'

But the orderly couldn't be by Monroe's side every

minute of the day. And one night all the forces in the universe colluded against Monroe.

He had dreamt again of his funeral. A green tarp. Four poles. Carter was shovelling dirt on his casket while his cell phone rang.

'Here,' he said to the rabbi. 'I've got to take this.'

Then he handed the shovel to the rabbi like a baton in a relay race. Turning his back, he flipped open his phone. Goldie's friends cocked their ears in Carter's direction. What else could they do? He was speaking so loud. He always spoke so goddamned loud, making wide swooping gestures with his arms. And such a suit! Silver pinstripes on black worsted wool, double-breasted with a nice narrow lapel. Monroe felt upstaged at his own funeral.

He woke up with a start. His heart was beating so violently that he looked down at his chest to see if the sheets were moving. And in those few moments while his head wasn't clear, when he wasn't quite sure if he was asleep or awake, he decided to take a leak. He forgot he was eighty years old. He forgot he was in the nursing home. Like he had done for decades, he swung his legs to the side of the bed, somehow vaulted over the side rails, and started walking to the bathroom. Five steps later, his hip gave out.

The call button around his neck landed between his shoulder blades. His arm was sandwiched between his bad hip and the floor. No matter how much he turned and twisted, Monroe couldn't find the leverage to get up. For eight hours he lay on the floor. Wardell found him the next morning.

'Anything feel broke? What were you thinking, man? What were you thinking?'

'I'm thinking we should get the hell out of here,' said Monroe. 'You and me. Skedaddle. Head for the highlands.'

It didn't take much for the orderly to lift him. Monroe must have weighed a hundred pounds.

'How 'bout I make a run to McDonalds? Bring us both back Quarter Pounders?'

'How 'bout if you shove that happy meal up your ass?' answered Monroe. Every bone in his body ached. He ran his hand up his legs and ribs, doing a quick inventory. 'I'm not kidding. I'm checking myself of out this dump. I checked myself in. I can check myself out.'

'How you know that?'

'The social worker – Maisy or Daisy, the one with the big tits – told me. There's a patient bill of rights, you know.'

His chin up in the air, Monroe tapped his fingers. He watched as Wardell tucked in the sheets extra tight. The old man could barely move, let alone contemplate another stroll. He grabbed the orderly's wrist.

'I mean it.' Monroe clung to that wrist like a life preserver and wouldn't let go. 'I'm leaving. Gonna get myself to the state of Washington and die on my own terms. Kaput! State-sanctioned and approved.'

He stared at the orderly and squeezed the wrist harder.

'You wanna come?'

Over the next several weeks, Monroe planned his journey. Maps were sprawled across his bed. Whether he was in the cafeteria or the hallway, the PT room or the lounge, he had a pen tucked behind one ear and a guidebook in his lap.

'There's no one you need to talk to about this?' asked Wardell. 'Your nephew? Your friends?'

'You see them lining up by my door?' asked Monroe.

'Paying me social calls? I've spoken to my attorney, Bob Finkle. He's arranging the video. He's getting a few shrinks to testify that I'm of sound mind and shitty body. Then we head to Seattle.'

He opened a joint bank account with Wardell and dumped a hundred grand into it. They bought an SUV with a V8 engine, top-of-the-line everything. Monroe took care of the paperwork and itinerary. The orderly took care of the rest.

Wardell knew his job was a dead end. Giving the nursing home notice was easy. Telling his mother goodbye was a lot harder. He sat her down by the kitchen table. His mother had cooked him his favourite foods. Roast chicken, scalloped potatoes. But everything tasted like metal lately. He made a mental note.

'It'll be for a year, tops. Me and Mr R. are going to see the country. The Grand Canyon. The Rocky Mountains. Then we're making our way through California and up the West Coast.'

His mother faced the sink, crying as she washed the dishes, her shoulders jerking, her voice gargling the words.

'And that old white man is paying you? This is one crazy idea, Wardell. This whole scheme is coated in crazy. You ever think of that?'

'Then at least he's seen Big Sur, Momma. And Monterey. And the sunrise over Sausalito.'

There was a lot more he wanted to tell her but couldn't. Two years earlier, he'd been diagnosed with the low blood. Pre-leukaemia they called it. Hell, it was supposed to stay like that for years. He only had to make it to Seattle.

'I'll try to call every week, Momma,' knowing it for a lie.

She was too poor to afford a computer or a fancy phone. Wardell looked at his mother one last time. Her apron had a lifetime of stains. Her lined face was a road map of heartache. There was a story behind each and every gray hair. And before he lost it, before the whole meal rose up in his throat, Wardell got out of his chair and left.

The trip took two months. They stopped in motel chains from one coast of the country to the other. The days flew by in a blur. They ate homemade rice pudding in twenty different diners and saw the world's largest ball of twine. Wardell pushed Monroe's wheelchair up the Continental Divide and wheeled it through the grand Mormon temple in Salt Lake City.

Some days they did nothing. At night, they each lay in their twin beds, the TV always blaring in the background. But the dreams not only persisted for Monroe, they became more detailed and intense. He followed the funeral procession from the cemetery to Carter's home just as if he were sitting in the limo beside him. He watched Abe Bernstein rinse his hands with a pitcher of water. Each of Goldie's friends daintily wrapped pastries in paper napkins before dropping them inside their purses.

'Maybe they're visions,' said Wardell. 'Like the Indians have. Or like that kid in the movie with the sixth sense.'

'He saw dead people. In this dream, only I'm dead. Everyone else is having a party! A fucking party! Counting my money on the way to the bank!'

It seemed no matter how hard he tried to escape the dreams, they followed him. He looked at Lake Mead and saw a mirror framed in black crêpe. When he gazed at the Montana horizon, all he saw was an endless tablecloth, rows of half-eaten bagels and lipsticked plastic forks. The flotsam and jetsam of life, thought Monroe, washing up on the shore.

San Francisco, they both decided, was their favourite city. They drove to Chinatown every night, sampling the dim sum from one small restaurant to the next. They never ate with the tourists. They'd peer inside storefronts and look for the places crowded with Asian faces, bustling with foreign tongues. They drove down Lombard Street, gassing the engine on the curves. And when they sat underneath the great redwood trees of Muir Woods, all they could think of was God.

'Do you think he exists?' asked Wardell.

He had brought them lunch. A dozen white takeout containers sat on a picnic table, the chopsticks still in them. They had feasted on leftover dumplings and eggrolls, gorging themselves on grease, the grease making its way down their chins and onto their shirts. While Monroe sat in his wheelchair, Wardell sprawled on the grass. He looked up at the tallest trees in the world and blew a long slow whistle between his teeth.

'If he exists, he's not paying attention most of the time,' Monroe said. 'Probably sitting up in heaven with a six-pack in one hand, a remote in the other, looking down during commercials.'

'And not all the commercials,' said Wardell. They were finishing each other's sentences now. 'Just the ones for women's products. Some of the others can be mighty entertaining.'

'Better than the TV shows,' added Monroe.

They gazed up at the treetops, looking upwards.

'Finkle said the papers are final. You're officially adopt-ed. Your mom okay with that?'

Wardell nodded. He hadn't spoken to his mother since they'd left Miami. He imagined her sitting at the kitchen table, opening the legal notice, her mouth wide.

'Maybe we should re-evaluate our options.' Wardell stood up and busied his hands, collecting the leftovers. 'Look how well you've been doing. Life's been good.'

He dumped the cartons into the bear-proof metal garbage can and folded the tablecloth neatly, following the creases as if it were a flag.

'I drove us here,' said Wardell. He wiped a tear before the old man could see it. 'I can drive us home.'

There was a hitch in the orderly's voice. A little hiccup of pain. Monroe glanced at Wardell. When a breeze brushed their faces, they both trembled. Then Monroe stared one more time at the sky.

'We still haven't tried the Ghirardelli ice cream place,' said Monroe. 'I think I may have one unclogged artery left.'

In Seattle, they checked into one of those all-suite motels that throw in a breakfast, a happy hour and a little kitch-enette. They bought groceries and magazines. Water and batteries. They even got new haircuts.

'We need to get ready!' Monroe bellowed. 'It'll be a long siege.'

Bandages and first-aid supplies. Cans and cans of tuna. Jars and jars of peanut butter.

'It's our final bunker,' said Monroe. 'Our Alamo. We need reinforcements.'

Finkel found them local counsel. There were legal papers, perhaps more videos, a consultation with a prescribing physician. In two months, tops, they would be ready. Monroe's will would be finalised and Wardell would be rich. Rich enough to buy his mother a house, rich enough to get a college degree. In two months' time they would be ready. They had a plan.

And then the nosebleeds started. One morning, Wardell had an infected hangnail. That night, there was a red line up his arm.

'I think I need to go to the hospital.' He rolled up his shirtsleeves. 'My blood problem. I think it's kicked into high gear.'

The old man stared at the arm. Wardell's hand was so swollen it looked like the skin would burst. Monroe reached over to touch it. All five fingers were hot.

A week later, Monroe had set up a new bunker at the Hutchinson Cancer Center. He appropriated a corner of the visitor's lounge, where he parked his wheelchair, a grocery bag of snacks, a pile of sweaters. They had stabilised Wardell and were searching the blood-marrow registries for a match. Monroe was frantic. All his life he had wanted a son and now he was slipping away. The doctors saw the old man in the halls and ran the other way. Each time he confronted them, the same conversation played out.

'My marrow's not good enough? Take all you want. Carve me open with Ginsu knives! Blast me with a bazooka!'

Whether it was a nurse or a doctor, the same response would follow. Loudly, because they thought the elderly were deaf. Slowly, because they thought the elderly were stupid.

'First of all, you're too old. Second, you're not a relative. Third, you'd have to match. The blood. It has to be a match.'

Monroe would yank his wispy hair in disbelief. Tufts stood straight out. Wasn't it obvious to everyone that he was the boy's father? The old man looked at the orderly and saw Goldie's smile, his father's hands, his mother's hopes. They had embarked – where was that writing pad? – on a journey and now life had sent them another detour.

First Wardell had to survive the transplant. The old man had seen plenty of pain in his life but nothing prepared him for the torture the boy endured. Each hour, then each day, then each week slowly passed. Six months later, they had reached their first milestone. Wardell's immune system was like a newborn's, the doctors told them. Gradually he would get stronger.

Monroe brought fresh food and laundered his clothes. Together, they went to the doctor's appointments and savoured each dollop of good news. The old man still had the visions. He saw them while he watched TV. He saw them on the sides of tall concrete buildings. He saw them spinning on the stop of the Space Needle. He saw them in the clouds.

But they were different now. Of course Carter was still whacking his breast. And Goldie's friends were busy making a great show of their grief. But now, in the front pew, sat the orderly. With a black ribbon pinned to his suit and a skullcap on his head, he whispered Monroe's name and chanted the ancient prayers. Tears ran down his cheeks. And Monroe knew that, in some small way, he would go on living forever.

3.
Not a Finger More
Shirley Fergenson

Richard dares me to do 'that banshee yodel' again. So I do. After I say no when he expects the opposite, after I call him a tyrant, after he pushes me just enough that I fall to the bottom of the basement steps, after I crash-land against the washing machine, I wail like a wounded animal. When he walks away, first making sure I am more frightened than injured – he is a doctor, after all – I stand, pick up the phone and call the police. While I wait, I pull the ring off my swelling finger before it is too late to remove it at all.

★

I had thought about leaving it in the safety deposit box before we moved to Costa Rica: my perfect blue sapphire surrounded by diamonds, a piece of night sky caught in a lasso of stars. But I couldn't. Richard gave it to me on our fifth anniversary, and I swore I would never take it off. That's why it was covered in yellow Nicaraguan dust that day I dangled my hand outside the window of our van. Richard, our four children and I were making this trip out of Costa Rica to extend our visas. An old, Costa Rican Peace Corps drop-out had told us that Panama was too risky for tourists, but Nicaragua was safe – war torn, but no longer

43

dangerous. Richard believed him, and I had to believe Richard. Cross the border, stay overnight, and return with a stamp that extended the deadline for another four months, like feeding a meter.

I was reading and translating out loud a sign in Spanish, PELIGRO, 'danger', watching the landscape morph from tropical to lunar, from lush coffee plantations hugging impossible cliffs to barren gullies beckoning to be filled – I hoped not with us – as we crossed the demilitarised zone into a country known for its contra rebels. The route was less road than a series of mouth-like craters waiting to rip and swallow the green gringos. Us. Richard gripped the steering wheel like a bronco-busting cowboy. Rugged, dark and laconic, his square chin and broad shoulders pulled me in and held me fast from the first. They still did. I bit my tongue when our van bounced into what could have been an excavation for a small skyscraper. Our children shrieked as if Disney had arranged this little treat for them. When the front tires found purchase on the other side, the van tilted crazily before righting itself again. Richard settled his nothing-to-worry-about grin on me. I swallowed the salty pocket of blood that had gathered in my cheek.

'Daddy, do that again.'

I turned to look at our youngest daughter, Laurie. Her chubby, pink face smeared with peanut butter, the only food she, Daniel, Chloe Kate and Julie would eat when we were travelling, if McDonalds weren't an option. I pulled a few sheets off our precious roll of toilet paper – we'd been told not to expect anything more absorbent than newspaper, if we were even that lucky – and swiped at Laurie's face while she bounced in and out of my reach.

Peanut butter, not rice and beans. How could I pack enough Skippy – or Charmin – for a year? That was my first innocent question that day, a few months after Richard had sold his orthopaedic medicine practice for so much money it felt like a super-jackpot lottery win. He had had a rough night and awakened agitated, excited.

'I had this amazing dream,' he said. 'We were drinking *papaya con leche* in Costa Rica on this porch with chickens and monkeys, all of us. But it wasn't a vacation. We were home.'

I wanted to say, 'Sounds more like an hallucination.' I did say, 'Maybe that was your subconscious telling you to find another job before we all end up like that crazy family in *Mosquito Coast*, blowing up an ice factory in some tropical rainforest.' I thought I got my refusal across with just the right amount of humour to pass. Richard didn't think I was funny.

Months passed. The vision moved from a fantastical dreamscape to a real reservation to have our van shipped on an empty banana boat from Wilmington, Delaware to Limon, Costa Rica. Daniel, our ten-year-old, threatened never to ride in the van again if there were even a hint of Chiquita left behind. When Richard asked the captain if he could accommodate our family along with the van – we would apprentice ourselves to the crew – the captain politely demurred, something about not having insurance for children. Daniel stopped gagging. I stopped laughing. Plane reservations were made. I helped the kids pack twenty duffel bags –half of them stuffed with books – and told my friends how excited and lucky I was to have this great opportunity, changing the subject when they asked me how

I really felt. It was only for a year. Besides, Costa Rica was famous for butterflies and orchids, no military and a good school system. Floridians event flew to San Jose for cheap elective surgery. How bad could it be?

We settled in Nicoya, Costa Rica's answer to the Wild West. I sent back letters filled with stories about scorpions in the bedroom, iguanas in the toilet and chickens in the kitchen. I said how cold showers could be really refreshing. I thought I was pretty funny and let Richard read my letters. He thought I was complaining – nothing funny there. I was re-educated with a two-hour monologue on family values. He did like the one about Maria, our next-door neighbour, who sent over *arroz con pollo* containing one of their few, precious chickens, because she said the *Americanos* were like helpless children who didn't know a plantain from a banana, and she didn't want to see the family go hungry.

I made one last swipe at Laurie's face, smearing rather than clearing the oily, tan spread that kept my daughter from starving. Back in Baltimore, this would have warranted a stop for soap, water and a paper towel or two. But now, clean enough.

'Daddy, make us go sideways again,' Laurie squealed into Richard's ear, her dimpled arm around his neck like a sausage necklace. He kissed her sticky fingers.

'Get back into your seatbelt, Baby Girl. I'll see what I can do.'

I looked over at my husband. His pulsing right temple told me what I needed to know: he was in charge; he would take care of us. Nothing to worry about. I loved that about him. I had gone from my parents' house to Richard's house with only a summer vacation between college and marriage, and neither my parents nor my husband wanted me to worry. I agreed with them. We drove on in silence, passing walled compounds topped with razor wire guarded by armed sentries. Nicaragua was not Costa Rica. Mostly we saw shacks with dusty bodies – difficult to differentiate rib-defined children and dogs – scrabbling together in barren yards. Every now and then an orange-and-gold lantana bush rose out of the jaundiced dust, like a lamp that had no visible power source.

'Daddy, I need to go pee,' said Chloe Kate, our seven-year-old.

'Cara, didn't I tell you to take them when we stopped at the border?'

That tone again. I turned my hand, palm up, and swiped my ring across my lap. It left a dirty streak, like a layer of itself, only the wrong colour, on my favourite pink skirt, the one that swished around my knees like an upside down tulip gone soft on its stem.

'I'm sorry. With all those kids begging around the car, I forgot. Maybe we can stop at the next town.' A bit of blue night-sky peeked out from between my fingers balled up in my lap. I must have been squeezing pretty hard, because when I unclenched, the ring had left behind a perfect pink imprint, like a negative. It matched my skirt.

He was quiet for a moment. Then, with a tight smile, he said loudly enough for the back seat to hear, 'You sound just like your mother with those damn excuses, Cara.'

'Daddy said a cuss word, Daddy said a cuss word,' Chloe Kate chanted, bouncing up and down, her stubby braids flying like small blond birds.

'Hey, CK,' Richard said, reaching back to tickle our middle

daughter, 'sometimes grown-ups say things to show how they feel. When you're twenty-one, you can use that word. Until then, it's only for Daddy.'

'How about Mommy? She's twenty-one.'

'I don't need words like that. I have other ways to share my feelings,' I told our daughter quietly.

'Yes, Mommy has other ways, don't you, Cara?'

Richard delivered his rhetorical question with his loaded eyes aimed at me, invisible to the back seat. I silently leaned away and looked out at a walled compound, almost elegant, except for odd circular pockmarks. I saw them on several more buildings, until the whole town seemed the victim of an unfortunate, scarring rash. I wondered if the random pattern was intentional, a native architectural statement, or the result of sub-standard, sandy concrete.

'Dad, look at all those bullet holes. Wow, there must have been some gigantic fight here,' Daniel said from the back seat.

Of course. Even my ten-year-old son recognised real life when he saw it. Goosebumps rose on my hot skin. This was the closest I had ever been to violence. By choice. No horror, car chase or war movies for me. When I was growing up, I had yearned for stories about choosing teams for canoe races across lakes with Indian names. Instead, I had heard about selections, wrong lines and camps where the prize was living another day. They probably didn't think I was listening. The closest I got to Frankenstein was with the Three Stooges as bodyguards. I even closed my eyes when Wile E. Coyote got flattened for the thousandth time by an Acme anvil.

The town appeared deserted as we drove through slowly, looking for somewhere to stop. I saw an open door leading to a jacaranda-shaded courtyard, full of children and adults celebrating something, maybe a birthday. I made eye contact with a black-haired woman whose smile disappeared as mine widened. I leaned out the window and, just as I was about to try out my Spanglish, her door slammed shut, as if it had been a mistake that it had been opened at all. We rode on in silence, except for Chloe Kate whining in the back about the heat. We circled the empty town square, looking for some sign of hospitality. There was none.

'We're going to press ahead to Managua,' Richard said. 'We'll get back on the road, and the kids can pee behind some bushes.'

'I don't want to pee in the jungle. What about scorpions?' Julie our oldest said. Ever since she found one in her favourite jeans on the laundry line – she had beaten it with the killing stick notched with her extermination count – Julie kept a strict vigil. She even built a cage out of a scrap of screen to protect her and her siblings' toothbrushes against ant nesting. Just like her father: see a problem, name it, face it, fix it.

Richard stopped. The kids piled out of the van with Julie beating the bushes. We sat in silence and watched our intrepid daughter lead her siblings, with fistfuls of wadded toilet paper, into the scrub. Back in Baltimore, they each had a private bathroom. They took bubble baths in a marble Jacuzzi. They had towel warmers. Julie would never have learned how to kill scorpions from me. There they were, a living tableau right out of their geography books. When they were finished, we pulled back onto the cratered highway. I reached over and massaged Richard's shoulder. Sometimes a touch helped.

'Daddy, I'm hungry, too,' Laurie wailed.

'Well, your mother shouldn't have given away your lunches, now should she?' Richard shrugged his shoulder out from under my hand. I didn't think he had seen me passing out our sandwiches to those begging kids at the border. His eyes were as hard and dark as the blacktop under our tires.

I reached into my bag, found a plastic spoon and handed it back to Daniel with a jar of peanut butter. 'Here, help your sisters with this. There's a jug of water in the back. This should hold you until we get to the hotel.'

I settled back into my seat, rested my cheek against the cool glass of the side window and closed my eyes. I had checked the map at the border. One main road traversed Nicaragua. Richard would get us to Managua without my navigating. A silly song Chloe Kate made up about 'Mommy reading maps backwards' buzzed through my head. I woke up with a headache to the sound of my children calling out answers to Richard's rapid-fire geography questions.

'Okay, give me the Great Lakes in order, west to east.'

Julie's and Daniel's voices tangled around my head.

'I know! I know! Let me have a turn! You answered last time!' Julie shouted.

I turned and saw Daniel clamp his hand over his older sister's mouth and with a gotcha smirk say, 'Lake Superior, Huron, Michigan, Erie, Ontario.' While he waited for Richard's praise, Julie ripped Daniel's hand off her mouth and crowed, 'You're wrong. Michigan comes before Huron. I guess you read maps backwards like Mommy.'

Richard laughed out loud.

I stretched my lips, not exactly a smile, and pretended it didn't bother me.

The rest of the trip passed in relative quiet. The closer we got to Managua, the more life we saw. A snarl of arms and legs, both animal and human, dangled off every kind of wheeled contrivance. Rooftop bus riders were perched so precariously that they might have been circus acts. I couldn't take my eyes off their nonchalant war against gravity. They needed to move, and they found a way.

Daniel's voice brought me back. 'Hey Dad, can we go there after we check into our hotel?' He was pointing to a sign VOLCAN MASAYA PARQUE NATIONAL. Lately, he had been interested in explosions, both man-made and natural – a short-lived phase, I hoped.

'I don't see why not, Dano.'

'I think we should find out if it's safe, first,' I said.

'It's a national park for God's sakes, Cara. You worry too much.'

'Yeah, Mommy, don't worry so much. We'll take care of you,' Laurie said in a mimicking voice. My face burned. My four-year-old was imitating Richard. My eyes and the top of my head were throbbing.

We drove into Managua. The Hotel International was an easy find. It was the only building taller than two stories still upright. I took no comfort in its verticality, the jagged crack running down its fake Mayan façade an almost perfect match for the lightning bolt cleaving my brain. Rubble bordered the hotel on three sides, the leftovers of a ten-year-old earthquake the country, in its war frenzy, hadn't had the resources to clean up. On the fourth side, elegant European-style villas housing foreign embassies stood incongruously intact.

After an expensive hotel lunch, Richard mumbled that he was paying the entire waitstaff's salary for the month.

We checked into a modern room with the kind of plumbing and electricity we had not seen since we left Baltimore. The children bee-lined for the television. Even Spanish soap operas looked good. Just as quickly, Richard turned it off.

'I thought you wanted to see a volcano. Who's ready?'

I got up from my chair slowly. What I really wanted was a warm shower and a nap in the cool, dark room, by myself. I turned to Richard. He cut me off as if he read my mind.

'Come on, the fresh air will do you good,' he said. I translated: he didn't want to take all the children by himself.

I reached for my purse. I remembered the armed guards we had passed on our way into the hotel. 'To keep the beggars out,' Richard had told me. I hooked the strap around the right side of my neck and under my left arm. We passed through the lobby. The concierge said the park was worth a visit and that we shouldn't have any problems there. I thought about leaving my ring and our cash and travellers' cheques in the hotel safe, but Richard said not to bother. We were safe. I looked out a side window at some almost-naked, stick-thin children playing in the rubble while their equally gaunt mother tried to sell single cigarettes to anyone leaving or entering the hotel.

We piled back into the van. Managua slipped past us like a child's block world knocked sideways by the class bully. But every now and then, a small new building stood up above the wreckage. We stopped at a kiosk for some cold Cokes and an orange Fanta for Laurie. A toddler wearing a rag of a diaper sat under a table, banging a spoon and kicking at a chicken getting too close to his toes. A small, wiry man, probably the father, was frying *empanadas* while his soft, round wife swept the concrete floor. I looked at my children, quiet and safe in the back seat. I looked at Richard. He was right. My headache was easing.

After about ten kilometres, dodging oxcarts, tractor-fronts, donkeys and bicycles piled high with ragtag riders precisely counterbalanced by bulging sacks – more circus acts – we pulled into the Masaya Volcano parking lot. A small armed guard, not much more than a boy, stopped us, and pointed out where to park. I frowned at Richard when I saw the crusty rifle he shouldered against his torn park-service t-shirt.

'See, don't you feel better now? This is the only entrance and exit and nobody's getting past him.'

I nodded, more to appease Richard than out of relief. I hugged my bag with our cash and traveller's cheques close to my ribs. Richard grabbed his bag with our passports and visas in one hand and scooped up Laurie with the other. Julie, Daniel, and Chloe Kate ran up the twisted stone stairway carved into the side of the volcano. The rise was so steep and sharp circling up into the low-hanging clouds that Rapunzel's castle could have peeked through the mist. I picked my way over loose lava rock, too slow to keep up with my scrambling children. Richard, with Laurie on his shoulders, passed me when I stopped to catch my breath. The wind was so strong that I saw rather than heard Laurie's squeal when a gust whipped my tulip skirt up to my chin, exposing me to a group of tourists on their way down. I gasped and laughed at how I would tell this one later: a Nicaraguan Marilyn-Monroe-over-the-steam-grate moment.

I finally reached the top. Knots of tourists were milling around the rocky plateau. Richard, with Laurie firmly in his arms now, motioned for me to come close. He was standing at the edge of the caldera. I craned my neck over the precipice and saw a very rough footpath leading down to a plateau full of stone letters about fifty feet below us. I caught Daniel's, Julie's and Chloe Kate's heads as they bobbed out from under an overhanging ledge.

'I told them it was all right to go down there and spell their names,' Richard said, pointing to the other tourists' volcanic graffiti. He almost had to shout, the wind was so loud. Laurie buried her face against her father's shoulder.

'Daddy, I want to go back to the car,' she wailed into his shirt. 'I don't like it up here.'

Richard hugged Laurie tightly to him and turned to me. 'You'll be all right. There's only one way up or down, and the guard's there.'

'Go ahead,' I said, the wind almost stealing my voice. 'I'll wait here for the kids.'

I watched Richard and Laurie begin their descent and noticed another couple leaving right behind them. I turned back to the caldera to keep an eye on my children. There were only two young men left on the plateau with me, locals by the looks of them, who might have been playing hooky from school. Some things are the same everywhere: a nice day, a long lunch, and before you know it, AWOL. I smiled at them and then turned to motion for the kids to finish and climb back up. I walked to the far side of the plateau to get a better look at the National Geographic view across the needle-sharp landscape stretching out below me.

Just then, one of the young men, the one who had smiled back, gestured frantically for me to come closer. I panicked, thinking maybe one of the kids had fallen. Before I took my second step, I felt a hard hand across my mouth and another around my waist. For a moment I relaxed. It must be Richard come back to surprise me, Laurie putting him up to this little game. Then I was on the ground, the smiler pinning me down. No game. I tightened my body as if it would make a difference. The other one cut my shoulder strap with a swift, accurate slice. I was an animal with nothing to lose. I thrashed blindly. My fingers gripped the already amputated bag at my side as I weighed my options: to give up our money or die or both. Then the blade flashed again so close to my mouth, I tasted dank metal at the back of my throat. I screamed into the wind. A hand moved the knife to my neck, where it delicately cut through a fine link in my gold-chain necklace. I felt fingers, not my own, touch my ring and pry my fist open. My hand was swollen. The ring was a blue ballooning aneurysm sprouting from my knuckle. The only way to get it was to take my finger. I stared at a hand that was attached to a wrist that was mine. The knife made a tentative move toward the ring.

'No, no, please, no,' I whimpered.

I lay perfectly still, transfixed. I wondered, in the time it took for the point of the blade to rest gently under the sapphire, how I would tell Richard that I lost the ring. I looked at the gaunt man-boy straddling me. Our terrified eyes met.

And I knew: this was his first time, too.

He dropped my hand and flicked the blade carefully between my watchband and my wrist. Not a scratch, and the watch was his.

The smiler was losing patience. He pulled his partner off and kicked me toward the edge of the caldera. I would not survive the drop.

I didn't want my children to see.

Oh. God. No. I live in Baltimore, Maryland, USA. The concierge said it was safe here. Richard promised I'd be safe. I squeezed my eyes shut. Pain was coming.

I don't know how long I waited to die. When I opened my eyes, the men had disappeared.

'Richard!' The wind swallowed my scream. I had come to rest at the cliff's edge, my hand dangling into the abyss. The ring remained embedded in my swollen finger.

★

Later I thought how desperation cushioned my attackers' flight, their thin-soled sandals no match for foot-slicing outcroppings. Later when I felt poetic rather than mugged, I heard the rocks in the caldera calling the sapphire back home. In the years after we returned to our estate overlooking Lake Roland, our children took to calling us Madre and Padre. When they talked about our time away, they described it as demarcated by the volcano: Madre, before and after. I knew what they meant.

In the beginning I told what I remembered. Then I left the story to my family. Their personal embellishments made heroes of whoever the teller was. Daniel and Julie both claimed they saw me first, when they climbed up out of the plateau and pulled me back away from the ledge. Chloe Kate said how she was the only one not afraid to go down the stone staircase by herself to get Padre. Laurie said how she saved her Padre by making him leave before the bad men came. Richard described his chase over the sharp-as-broken-glass terrain, with shots fired by both him (with a borrowed pistol) and the armed guard, like a scene from *Raiders of the Lost Ark*.

There were things I did not tell. Some days I felt hands on my neck. Some days I wondered who got our dollars: the man-boy's family, maybe a baby sister or brother, a grand-mother? Some days I felt so light, a good, strong wind could have carried me away. The children stopped singing the reading-maps-backwards song. Richard called me hard and guarded because I looked directly at him and sometimes said no.

One day I said no at the wrong time. He was talking at me in our bedroom. One hour. Two hours. Three hours. He had so much to say about how disappointed he was: why I didn't trust him, why I didn't respect him, why I wanted to get a job now that the children were growing up. I should have wanted to be with him. And there was so much yard work to do. We could do it together. Except for the months that he was in the Congo doing his medical philanthropy.

If I were working, who would pick up the black walnuts all over the property that the squirrels wanted to bury in his newly seeded lawn, all four acres of it?

'I bet Phil and Hugh next door will be happy to earn some spending money,' I said.

And who would keep the wood stove going?

'Turn on the furnace until I get home,' I said.

It was getting dark and late, dinner time. Laurie and Chloe Kate were downstairs pretending we were 'in conference', which was Richard's way of telling them that he want-ed me all to himself. Daniel and Julie were away at college.

'Madre, we're hungry,' Laurie called up the stairs. 'When's dinner?'

Finally. Saved.

'I'll be right down, honey.'

I headed toward the doorway. Before I could ask if she wanted rice or noodles with her chicken, Richard jumped in front of me.

'Madre and I aren't finished with our conference, Baby Girl. You and CK can get a snack.'

'I don't want a snack, I want dinner,' Chloe Kate whined up the stairs. Her intolerance for delayed gratification was legendary.

'Do what I said. Madre will come down when she's ready.' Richard enunciated each word.

Silence downstairs. Even Chloe Kate knew better than to try again. I sank back.

He planted his feet in opposite corners of our bedroom door and reached to the upper corners with his hands.

He was an X. A fill-in-the-box next to your selection X.

I watched him and, for a crazy moment, wanted to believe he was stretching.

'I'd like to finish this conversation later, after dinner,' I said, as if I were asking a friend to call me back later. Because I was busy. No big deal. Nice and easy. I moved toward him and judged the space between his elbow and his knee.

'No, Cara, I want to finish now. I'm not really hungry yet. You're not, either.'

If I bent down and hunched my shoulders, I could just squeeze through because of how his right hip was canted.

I made my move.

My head grazed his forearm.

I was in trouble.

'You shouldn't hit me like that, Cara.'

He dropped both arms, grabbed my neck and shoulders

and pushed. Hard. I missed the foot of our sleigh bed. Just. I watched myself fall and land on the thick plush of a rose-and-lily-bouquet rug we bought together in Manhattan. Madison Avenue. Aubusson, I think. On my way down, the flowers looked so silky I almost didn't think to break my fall, and then I was surprised at the abrasions on my elbows.

There was more. I felt other hands. On me. On my neck. Around my waist.

Boy-man hands.

I was above the caldera, and if I didn't scream for help with all my might, the wind would lift me and carry me over the edge, like a bird without wings, and I wouldn't wake up because this was not one of those dreams.

My bedroom, my house, my world filled with a terrible sound. It was coming from me. Five minutes . . . fifteen . . . sixty. I didn't know how long. I heard a keening harmony from downstairs. I stopped. Richard was standing over me.

'You're scaring the girls. I didn't push you that hard. Stop screaming. You sound like a banshee yodeller.'

I stopped. His face was a mask, stretched and discoloured like something spoiled, waiting to be thrown away. He ran down the stairs, and I heard murmuring, comforting sounds breaking through the miasma that was my daughters' fear. I pulled myself up, like a dog, on all fours, panting. If I could make it downstairs, they would see I was all right. With legs that felt as if at any moment they would return to dog position, I let myself circle, slide and slip down my winding staircase, where a lucky girl could have floated in her wedding gown toward her waiting Prince Charming.

Richard was standing, hugging and comforting Laurie and Chloe Kate, telling them I was fine.

'I need to apologise. I want to apologise,' he said. He reached out to include me in his circle of love. Chloe Kate and Laurie looked at me sideways, to see how fine I was. I was so stunned at the impending apology – Richard never apologised to me – that I gave my daughters a nod of confirmation.

'Girls, I'm so sorry Madre and I scared you. Madre didn't mean to scream so loud. We were having a disagreement, that's all. Everything's going to be all right. You know how much we love you.'

He stopped talking, and tears – real tears – puddled, spilled and left glistening tracks down his grey, drawn cheeks. I didn't know why he was crying. Laurie and Chloe Kate were probably crying from relief. My eyes were dry.

★

I am ashamed that my first banshee yodel was not enough to send me packing. When I'm sitting at the bottom of the basement stairs, when I finally call Richard by his name, when I'm terrified Laurie will think this is what a wife looks like, I see a passing oxcart that appears full, but I make room. I pile on my favourite blue leather recliner, my books, and, of course, Laurie, the only one left at home. I take what I need, not a finger more.

But something is not right. In spite of my small load, my balance is off. I know immediately what it is.

I throw my piece of night sky caught in a lasso of stars into Lake Roland. The circus is waiting. No sequinned leotard. No safety net.

4.
Janus: A Path to the Future
Nod Ghosh

It was a Sunday when you told me you'd decided to transition from male to female.

After more than half a lifetime together, it can't have been an easy revelation. Your anxiety showed in the way you twisted your hands, wrapping them one around the other, like you were washing a sheet. It wasn't clear if we'd be travelling the same route together, or whether we'd met a fork in the road. You'd go your way and I'd go mine. But you invited me to share the journey, if I wanted to. I did.

You had genuine fears about how the world would accept a six-foot-one 'tranny'. You worried for our children, and how other people would perceive them: fatherless, with two mothers. You delayed telling them until we could meet face to face. By that time, you had started on testosterone blockers and were wearing oestrogen patches. Your hips were filling out, and you'd managed to prang the car whilst reversing out of a supermarket car park. Some things hadn't changed. You'd always cried more readily than I did when watching sentimental films.

You had concerns about the world of employment, the uncertainty about fundamentals that provide a *raison d'être*

and put bread on the table. Your livelihood could potential-
ly be eroded by insidious prejudice or overt bigotry. We
made two lists of friends, family and colleagues. One
included those we guessed would accept the change. The
other was for those who would likely shy away. Ultimately,
not everyone slotted into their anticipated category. We lost
some acquaintances as we journeyed along the precipitous
route, and we gained others. But, in those early days, it was
the fear of the unknown that haunted me.

You wondered if I would still love you. I speculated
about whether you'd still want me, or whether you'd be
attracted to men once your hormonal profile changed. I'm
more epicene than ladylike, but perhaps my hair-speckled
chin and I-don't-give-a-toss attitude wouldn't be enough. It
took a while to learn that gender identity and sexuality were
independent variables.

On the flight to Belgium to see 'Dr Bart', I reflected on
how long I'd known your internal woman. Bart was going
to perform the first surgical procedure of your transition:
facial feminisation. There were too few surgeons in New
Zealand who specialised in that area, so we'd had to look
overseas. The surgical plan sounded like something from a
horror film. Amongst other things, it involved peeling back
the skin of your forehead, flattening the male bony bossing
at the eyebrow, shaving a few centimetres from your jaw-
bone, and transplanting flesh from your abdomen onto
your lips. He would be like a sculptor, hewing a woman out
of a male rock exterior – the woman I'd always known you'd
harboured within.

When we got together thirty years earlier, I was aware of
a powerful female element to your psyche. You kept Her

hidden from friends, family and colleagues. You wouldn't generally appear in public wearing a dress or in full make-up, unless copious amounts of alcohol were involved. At fancy-dress parties, other stubble-chinned males in dresses commented how well you carried yourself as a woman, whilst they fluffed up their artificial bosoms and flounced voluptuous wigs. They wouldn't make anything more of it, as the conversation veered towards rugby, cars, mountain biking and other areas within the male domain. But we'd be glad to give Her an outing. She was comfortable at home, with only the two of us around. For years I thought that was all She needed.

Flying from New Zealand to Europe is a slow process. There are many air miles one can give over to thinking. As we landed in Dubai, I looked at the segmented building and thought about how your decision to transition had come as a bolt from the blue for so many. I had hoped that others would have glimpsed Her over the years – something in your eyes or your stance that revealed your femininity, without the need for ballet flats or mascara. I had hoped they'd have seen what I'd seen. But it seems no one had.

Through the years, you readily took on female roles, but what rational male of our generation wouldn't? You were not the type to be reticent about shopping, cooking or child rearing. You made baby clothes for nephews and nieces, and took several years out to be the house-parent when our own children were born. But you'd still go to the pub with the lads, partake in extreme sports and appreciate an attractive woman as much as other guys. You may not have been an archetypal ultra-masculine man, but you wore your male totems and jumped through the appropriate boy-hoops.

We started telling people about your transition in late 2012. That New Zealand summer seemed to burn on for months. It was a slow and cautious rollout, a hierarchy of friends and relatives that had to be told in a specific order, to avoid hurting someone because they'd been told after others in the wider circle. The careful orchestration required many late-night phone calls to our native UK, so brothers and sisters would receive the news simultaneously. Revealing your plans to elderly relatives was especially daunting.

'Do you remember when I was a kid and I used to insist I was really a boy?'

'I remember you always said *ki korbo*? Always asking what to do next.'

My eighty-four-year-old father was a little hard of hearing and very adept at changing the subject.

'Yeah. I know I bugged you and Mum all the time. Sorry about that.'

I tried to get back on track. The long-distance call was punctuated with random whistles and purrs, making it even harder for Dad to hear me.

'Yeah, but remember I was always saying I was a boy and refused to wear dresses?'

'Mum used to . . .' and he was off in a different direction again, reminiscing about my dead mother.

'Yeah, but about the boy thing. There are some kids that really are that way. They don't grow out of it. They go on to have sex changes.'

'Is it evening there?'

'Yeah, nine twenty New Zealand time. Must be eight twenty in the morning for you? But you've heard of sex changes, right?'

As a rule, my father was uninterested whenever I talked

about you. There was a certain amount of history there. Fathers rarely think their daughters' partners are good enough for them. I was about to throw a can of petrol on that fire. I persevered. The phone carried on making its odd whirring and buzzing sounds.

After fifteen minutes, I asked him if he understood what I'd said.

'No,' he replied, and carried on talking about something entirely unrelated. It fell to my siblings to break the news to him, and to deal with his shock and anxiety.

Telling our colleagues proved a little easier. We chose the day after the marriage-equality bill passed its third reading in New Zealand's parliament. There was a lot of discussion on the subject, and a strong feeling of support in many circles. We celebrated the fact that we wouldn't have to have our marriage annulled. You baked me a cake, which I shared with my workmates.

We landed in Charles de Gaulle Airport in Paris on a Friday, thirteen days before you were due to go under the knife. Leaving our luggage at the Gare d'Austerlitz, we walked through Le Jardin des Plantes. Wandering through the uniformly pruned plane trees that vaulted over our heads, I saw you smile. Soft drizzle dusted our faces as we looked at polygons of grey light filtering through the branches. You reminded me we'd walked through these same gardens in the 1980s with our one-year-old daughter. As we walked hand-in-hand, we contemplated how she would cope with this monumental step. She was struggling with the changes. Naturally close to her stay-at-home father, she had an immense feeling of loss. I'd tried to explain that you were still you. Different, but the same. Less strength in your upper body, but more articulate. Still able to share all the same memories, but so much happier – not living a lie. I dropped your hand, self-conscious, not yet bold enough to parade my new gayness with confidence.

We found a cafe, shared a beer. The block opposite held apartments, four stories high. Occupants had placed ornate rows of topiary, like regiments of neat soldiers, on the tiny balconies. You commented on how full the air was, full of the shouts of invisible people, and the sharp smell of unknown solvents. Sometimes all we can hear in our New Zealand home is the plangent call of dairy cows and the soft sound of our own breathing. The air is tinged with the brash green fragrance of a freshly mown lawn, or the smell of hissing rain on the hot rock of the Port Hills.

We walked along the Seine towards Notre Dame. I took photos of you posed beside hulking sculptures – some of the last pictures of your familiar face before it was altered forever. The discordant clang of bells from a smaller church pierced the air. We came across the Pont des Arts. The sun poked through the clouds and picked out the glint of shining metal as we approached the bridge. Had I known of the tradition of engraving a padlock with lovers' names, I would have got one made with your newly chosen name carved next to mine. Another lock to add to the thousands packed tightly on the grill of the pedestrian bridge. Not everyone approves. It brings to mind the bra fence in Cardrona, in Central Otago, New Zealand. People loved or hated the collection of bras that appeared in the late 1990s. There were hundreds of them. The council cleared them in 2006. I've heard a rumour the bras have recently reappeared. I will take you there one day, and we'll leave a bra each.

We talked about our hopes and fears over a sashimi meal, before racing on the TGV to Reims. Every time we see old friends, there is a process to go through. You first met Sophie in the mid-1980s, whilst busking in Paris with friends from the North of England. She was married to an American at the time. A group of you played music and drank into the small hours every night. Then you'd hit the Metro in the afternoon. A bunch of guys with amps, guitars and drums that you'd lug onto train carriages along with your voices. You'd play Irish jigs and reels mixed with a collection of homemade songs.

Sophie was waiting for us in her silver car at the station. There was that look of uncertainty in her eye, a certain hesitance. I've seen that look numerous times over the months. A questioning stance that asks, 'Is my friend still there?' You still had the same face, but modified by the unmistakable trappings of femininity. Light make-up and dangly earrings. You are one of those lucky transgender women who still have their own hair. There are those who opt to only go so far down the path of change, avoiding surgery or hormone therapy. Others embark on it too late in life. Some end up with the round dome of male pattern baldness. Unlike birth women with alopecia, or those undergoing cancer chemotherapy and radiation treatment, trans women are destined to wear wigs or hats – it is difficult to 'pass' as female with a hairless head, when other subtle differences belie a male origin.

We stayed with Sophie, her partner and son for a few days. Over that time, the uncertainty disappeared, and the laughter resounded as it always had. We walked through Reims, scrutinising the ninth-century cathedral with critical tourists' eyes. Sophie told us Muslim scholars had been brought in to calculate the forces the vaulted ceilings could withstand, and to design the flying buttresses characteristic of architecture from that era. Apparently the cathedral was never completed. Some of the spires are missing. We walked sedately amongst the throng of visitors, four adults, reading plaques about King Clovis and Joan of Arc. Sophie's eight-year-old son ran ahead of us, chirping like an excited bird, running in and out of cubbies and between the pews, causing an unholy riot in the sacred space.

We ranked the stained glass windows in order of preference. Sophie rated the blue Marc Chagall window. She pointed out the painterly figurines to her youngster, coaxing him to stand still for three or four seconds. I captured Imi Knoebel's geometric designs with my camera: bold blue, red and yellow panes projecting shafts of cobalt or blood red onto the stone slabs of the church floor. You liked the sea-green and grey windows that flanked images depicting local champagne production.

Before leaving France, we visited Sophie's aging mother, Alice. The ravages of dementia had taken her mind. Initially, Sophie was reluctant to take us. She wasn't sure how to explain your transition to her mother. I recalled my conversation with my father and was sympathetic. However, when we bought flowers for her to give her mother, she relented and said we should take them ourselves.

Alice perceived that someone she once knew was visiting. Her smile spoke volumes when you pressed the flowers into her hands. She practiced a few sentences of English. The old lady was still in the family home she'd occupied for decades. The garden was overgrown to the point where it was impenetrable, shrubs more than four metres high poking towards the sky – a gardener's nightmare or a magical a maze for an eight-year-old. Pictures of Charles Aznavour and Picassos forged by Sophie's late father were scattered over the walls.

I felt a shiver of familiarity when I walked into the room we'd stayed in years earlier, in 1999. Memories flooded back. A total eclipse of the sun was to be visible from a tract of land that cut through the south of England and parts of Europe. Our children were young. A picnic on a hill. Streams of people climbing up, carrying hampers. Excited chatter in French and broken English. We sat and waited. Champagne glasses clinked. We hoped the clear skies that had emerged that morning would remain long enough for the show. The light developed an eerie quality until, eventually, the sky darkened. You held my hand. The children looked on in awe as cows lay down and sparrows began to roost. A shadow raced across the land. We peered through our sun-filtering glasses as a textbook corona formed, a fiery golden ring.

You came and found me, shook me out of my reverie. It was time to go.

We spent another day in Paris, visiting the Louvre and the Centre Pompidou, feasting on a plethora of iconic art we could only dream of in New Zealand. There followed a week in the UK, visiting friends and family. I wondered how you felt when you faced everyone, people who would be seeing you in your female form for the first time. It was like replaying what had happened in France over and over again. You coped well, though the effort of explaining everything about transition was a little wearing at times for both of us.

Two days before you were due to be transformed, we took the Eurostar to Ghent. A short taxi ride from the station brought us to a haven called 'Garden in the City'. A married gay couple who welcomed people in your situation owned the place. Beyond the hustle and bustle of the street was a garden with pots of vibrant flowers. Vines cascaded down the side of the flat at the end of the garden. It would be our home for a few days. Mr Tom and Diego, the two resident cats, wandered aimlessly in and out of the apartment.

That evening we walked on the riverside and made our way to the historical quarter. Buildings with crenulated façades flanked the river. Some had their construction dates displayed on plaques. Multi-storey seventeenth-century edifices teetered like sandcastles. They used to build tall and narrow, apparently because of the prohibitive building taxes on the waterfront. We walked nervously past brick walls with visible bulges. Coming from a region so recently devastated by earthquakes, we were a little cautious. But nothing moved.

The next day, we visited Gravensteen, the eleventh-century castle in Ghent built by Philip of Alsace. Inside was a museum displaying torture devices. The local judiciary had been located in the castle in the past, and the various spikes, shackles and straitjackets had been used not only to control criminals, but also to restrain people with 'mental illnesses', including epilepsy. I wondered what would have happened to people with gender dysphoria in the thirteenth century. The dank basement with its beaten-earth floors had a residual stink of terror. Pools of water from the river seeped in through the walls. I thought it prudent to get out of there before the haunting image of a circular, halo-shaped device encrusted with sharp spikes reminded you too powerfully of what was about to happen to you.

We sat by the river sharing Belgian chocolates.

'Are you scared about the surgery?' I ventured.

'A little.'

'What worries you most?'

'Nerve paralysis.'

I pulled a face, mimicking someone who'd lost control of their facial muscles. A line of chocolaty drool dripped onto my knee.

'Not supportive.'

I snapped my lips back into position.

'And what do you fear most after that?'

'That it won't do what it says on the tin, that I'll come out of it still not looking feminine.'

'And you can't realistically assess the results for nearly a year?'

'No. At least that long for the swelling to settle and for everything to fall back into place.'

Swarms of beautiful young things passed us. Ghent is a 'young' city, with several universities and colleges. We wondered what had happened to all the ugly ones. Perhaps they'd all been to visit Dr Bart, and had had their ugliness ironed out of them. Yellow-helmeted workers were erecting a pontoon across the river for the Ghent Festival, which would take place in a few days.

'Do you care if you don't turn out beautiful?'

'I'm fifty in ten days.'

'So it doesn't matter?'

'That's the sad thing, you see. It does.'

'You'll always be beautiful to me.' I squeezed your knee.

'Then you're not a very objective judge.'

'No, I didn't mean it like that.'

'You see, I think *you're* gorgeous, but when I think about it objectively . . . well you're a bit of a dog.'

'Fuck off! Here, wanna share the last chocolate?'

I wanted you to enjoy the sensation of taste. To savour the creamy delights we'd spent fifteen minutes selecting at the chocolatier's. You'd be eating baby food for the next week.

After you left for Dr Bart's clinic on the Thursday, I let Diego curl up on my lap and have a sleep. I pummelled and kneaded his sleek fur, and tried not to think about what was happening to you. It didn't work. How much do we fall in love with the image a person's face projects? I thought about articles I'd read about burns victims who'd had plastic surgery and then didn't recognise themselves, even when surgeons had performed technical miracles. Would you still feel like you? How much does the way you look matter? How much would you change because of what was happening to you?

I visited the museum of fine art to distract myself. That didn't work either. I moved our belongings to the next apartment we'd be staying at, one more suited to post-operative needs. I was like an expectant father, pacing, waiting for the moment I could stop worrying and light that cigar. I shopped, and filled the fridge with puréed mush and ready-made smooth soups for when you came out. Eventually it was time to catch the bus to Kortrijksesteenweg, where Dr Bart had his clinic. I arrived at 7.30 PM as instructed, but wasn't allowed to see you straight away. I tried to fight off the hollow feeling that had been churning inside me all day. I knew it would only disappear when I was able to see you, intact and alive.

Although you were disorientated and claustrophobic behind your water-filled face-cooling mask, you still managed to grunt a few words. Your face looked visibly shorter, in spite of the inflammation. I didn't stay long, figuring you needed to rest. Lost in my thoughts on the bus back to the apartment, I managed to miss my stop. A combination of inattention, and my rudimentary French meant I ended up in the next city. My usual sense of adventure had abandoned me. I wanted to be back in our temporary home. I got a train and taxi back.

I returned to Kortrijksesteenweg late on Friday morning to accompany you back to the apartment. You seemed to have recovered massively overnight, though it may have been an illusion, as you were wearing your own clothes instead of the blood-soaked gown I'd seen you in the day before. Your forehead was stretched tight with inflammation, and you didn't recognise yourself in the mirror. In the apartment, I was kept busy reapplying cold packs to your face every forty minutes, trying to coax you to take teaspoons of fluid, making sure you had your medication on time, helping you to the bathroom, and keeping you from getting bored when you weren't sleeping. It wasn't a romantic holiday, but I was glad we were together and pleased I could do something of practical use.

That night, Etienne and Gina, who owned the complex we were staying in, were entertaining in the courtyard outside our apartment. I poked my nose through the curtains and saw people sharing bottles of wine, laughing and enjoying elaborate courses of food that were brought out of the kitchen. I looked at the half finished, liquidised gruel in your bowl. It was streaked with blood.

You woke in the middle of the night, eyes swollen with sleep and surgical intervention, hair curving in random directions. The disorientation that accompanies dreams cloaked your words. There was desperation in your voice as you described your dream to me. You seemed delirious, though your skin was cold to touch. You spoke of a dog the size of your little finger. You followed it into a dream garden and found finger-sized apes lolloping in the grass. You couldn't form hard consonants like 'p' and 't'. They came out as sibilant whimpers. I asked you to repeat several phrases. It took a long time, and you needed to write some of it down. But it seemed important to get it out.

That is when I realised the value of having someone who cares about you when you are recovering from surgery. If I hadn't been there, you could have paid to have a nurse visit you daily. It may have even been possible to find someone to take a night shift, to ensure you weren't alone if anything untoward happened. You wouldn't have had someone to laugh with you, however, and share the simple joy of an absurd dream. That can only come from someone who knows you, someone who wants to know about the phantasmagoria that haunts you at night.

There was a cemetery next to the apartment. I walked there mainly for exercise, but I was also curious about what people chose to mark the resting places of their loved ones. It was a huge graveyard, inundated with little, round worm casts that made me think of subterranean creatures having a party in that nutrient-rich environment. By Sunday, you were ready for a small walk. I took your arm, led you to my favourite spots. You cried when you saw little graves marked with plastic windmills and rain-choked teddy bears. I showed you the graves with what appeared to be just-in-case breathing holes, small chimney-like vents by the sides of the plots. I assumed they were there for people who were afraid of being buried alive, but I didn't know for sure. There were a lot of them.

You slept a lot for the next week and discovered that ice cream was quite soothing. It was a useful addition to the soups and liquidised mush I'd been feeding you. I was keen to find nutrient-dense foods to help build you up again.

Whilst you slept, I explored the canals and watched water rush in through the sluice gates. I went running through an industrial zone, following a sign that said CUPRO CHIMIQUE, assuming it would be a copper smelter. A mountain of metal distracted me: a collection of discarded parts for recycling. Curls, spikes and tangles, some rusted, some not, formed a mound two to three stories high. It seemed like millions of unidentifiable items were competing to poke through the surface. Distant plumes of smoke curled up into a clear sky.

Unused train tracks ran parallel to the road. A little further on, I saw an abandoned train with little trees growing on the carriages. I got back to the apartment to find you'd just woken from another vivid dream.

With the help of a piece of paper and sign language, you explained how you'd been coaching three-year-old Russian basketball players in your sleep. The children in your dream referred to you as The Duchess. It seemed really important to you that you get all the details correct, despite your difficulty forming words with your torn, swollen mouth. Even with the inflammation, you had the wide-eyed look of a child who had woken from a vivid dream. You gripped my hand as you described leading the children down nauseatingly steep steps with a sheer drop on one side. In the dream, you were alternating man-woman-man-woman-man-woman-man. The scene shifted to your workplace. People were treating you as female, referring to you as 'she', but using your old, male name. I guessed there would be a lot of dreams like that over the next months.

You'd made arrangements with the HR department to return to work as your female persona. Despite our anxieties about how a large organisation would deal with your situation, their conduct had been exemplary. An appropriate email had been composed and sent to all the relevant people. Name badges and uniforms had been prepared, so you'd be able to return to work after the recovery break as 'she'.

On Tuesday, you had your post-op check with Dr Bart. In the waiting room, we met someone who was about three days ahead of you in the procedure. She'd come from Austria and spoke clear English, so she was able to give us an idea of how things would progress over the following few days. The fact that she was able to speak clearly was more exciting than the fact that she could speak English. That night, we shared a beer to celebrate the fact that your recovery was progressing as it should. I sipped a dark Kasteel Donker, my first beer in a week. I'd been keeping you company in abstaining from alcohol. We were both a little dizzy after one small glass of the malty brew. I squinted at the small print on the label and discovered it contained 11 percent alcohol. We didn't open a second bottle.

It was your birthday on Friday. I gave you a card and a massage. There was no present, as I planned to get you something when you were feeling a bit better. We left Ghent that day. We planned to go back to the UK so you could recover with family. We were due to take the Eurostar from Brussels. It was a skin-fryingly hot day.

We took the opportunity to visit the Atomium in Heysel. The iconic building opened in 1958 for Expo 58, that year's World's Fair. It consists of nine aluminium-coated spheres joined by struts, in a formation that is supposed to represent an atom of iron. There were exhibits of 'modern' 1950s paraphernalia, including souvenirs from the time. The Atomium was originally created to promote the use of atomic energy, in an era when we were even less aware of its long-term problems and uncertainties than we are now. (Half of Belgium's power comes from nuclear power stations.) We took the stairs up to the restaurant, where we had a drink and looked out over the city. A *son et lumiere* show in one of the spheres delighted us, lights projected onto a multi-faceted sculpture in the centre of a dark room. Another sphere housed sleeping pods for children on overnight school trips.

Saturday didn't bring you the rest and recovery you needed. My sister hosted a family reunion. It was the first time you'd got together with your brother and sister for more than eleven years. All families have skeletons in proverbial cupboards, and ours was taken out and given a good kicking that day. It was time for forgive and forget – and, by the way, your brother is now your sister, be nice and say hello. It is always the people who are closest that are affected the most by major change, so we were prepared for some raw emotions about your transition.

My sister glued together all the factions with the best adhesive of all: food. Her dining table groaned under the weight of twenty curries. I'd made a cake. Your siblings were reserved to start with. My brother-in-law made tentative moves between watching football with the guys, and sitting between both his sisters in the garden. A sweltering sun beat down onto reddened shoulders. Your sister took a small cloth bag out of her purse and gave it to you. Inside was a tiny wristwatch. It had been your mother's. Two toddlers, one from your family the other from mine, skirted around each other, avoiding one another with careful precision. The adults, however, had reconnected. We were pleased but exhausted at the end of the day.

That was nearly a year ago. Not long after the reunion, we returned to New Zealand. Your wounds slowly healed, people became accustomed to using your new name. We launder your work uniforms, and there are skirts and blouses rather than trousers and shirts. I carry a drawing in my handbag of a specific type of vibrator recommended by the psychologist. I haven't ventured into a sex shop to purchase one. I can't see that it would offer any benefits over the one we already own. We are not perfect, we fight and bicker like any other couple. We laugh a lot too.

You will have completed a year of living in your new gender by July, eligible for the next stage. The recommendations have been made, and the psychologist and endocrinologist have forwarded letters. You are undergoing another round of pre-operative blood tests and X-rays. You have asked me if I'd be prepared to use my annual leave to accompany you to Thailand for your surgery. I have said yes.

After more than thirty years, love has evolved into an unseen entity that beats steadily through my life, like cardiac tissue. I don't have to think about whether I actively love you, any more than I have to plan blinking or taking my next breath. It is as automatic as peristalsis and as enduring as the rocks that surround us in the Port Hills.

5.
Enfolded
Catherine McNamara

All along she called him Gerard. It was not his name. When the game ended, she stayed Mariam for a while, but he would slip. She enjoyed calling him Gerard, partly because that game had tickled them both so hard, and now it was a kind of trace. There was another game where she was O and he was M, but that was a sexual game, grinding and full of spluttered words, burrowing and friction. There were no games now. She sat on her suitcase at his local airport, waiting for the driver they would send, because he had fallen from a ladder and lost the use of his legs. He couldn't piss, he said. Couldn't drive. Couldn't have an erection.

There had been no need to say that. She notes a young man heading her way from the car lot.

At the house, he is dressed for her, wearing a printed shirt she had bought for him when they were together, three decades ago. He wears this shirt every time they meet. Winter in Amsterdam, summer in Sydney, spring in Addis. Always this shirt. At first she stands a few metres away from him. The room is messy. A creative man's disorder. She sees that crankiness has just left his face and his chin juts out, raised, ever-searching. He lifts an arm that has become womanish. His fingers are lean, reptilian, nails bitten to the core.

She takes his hand, feels the cool pads envelope her sticky digits. She folds to her knees and cries in his lap. It smells of an old man's trousers, old man's urine.

The same young man pushes his wheelchair out to the patio. Before following, she removes her espadrilles and feels her feet embrace the tiled floor, a kiss on the tarmac. She looks at her bent toes, black nail polish. It hits her that he can't feel his anymore, he has to look at them like dirty mementos in a house-girl's soapy hands. She remembers his toenails scratching her in bed, his knees cool behind her knees. She smells food: the ponderous palm-nut soup she hasn't eaten in an age.

She hears his summoning from outside. If anything, his voice booms louder now. Perhaps because he feels imprisoned? But he has always snapped at her, snapped at most people. Her views of him have not yet shifted from able to disabled. She thinks of centaurs. The upper body fused to another creature, the surging of the arms, the tossing of the head and neck. She remembers sweat clinging to the fine hairs of his chest, the taste of it. She thinks his smell has altered.

It is a shock to see how crowded the yard has become. The palms lofty above the rooftop. No one has cut them. His fingers plunge into the red soup, wear a glove of its viscous colour.

'Sit down.' He points to her. 'You know I hate to eat cold food.'

The young man uncaps her beer. She sits down. The soup steams. The scent reaches into her. The sea, too, sends her tendrils through the dusty, clacking leaves. It's not far from here. The veranda rails are rusty. Chunks of concrete have fallen off, landing in soft dirt below where, she hears, there are children. Are they his children? Begotten long before he fell to the ground here? A friend – Nana Yaw – had said there were dozens of them, an unchecked, almost tribal reproduction. But Nana Yaw had a bitter tongue.

'You don't look any different,' he says to her.

She raises her eyebrows and looks out. Once, they were accomplices. Now she wonders about the smell coming from his trousers and whether the young man takes him to pee or there is a bag for it. And whether this mercy mission is going to include sitting on the loo all night after downing his cook's food.

'Not used to this anymore?'

'Not really,' she says. 'But I'll give it a go.'

He pushes his plate away, half-eaten, and drinks his beer from the bottle. She thinks he drinks a lot of beer sitting here. He has a paunch. He watches her wash her hands and begin the soup.

'You know I like to watch you eat.'

He stares at her; he has often stared at her. Occasionally, her eyes cross his. Long ago, she begged him not to make a study of her, an understanding of each flinch of her nerve-endings. He once wrote a poem to her nipple. 'Morning nipple, mid-morning nipple, my nipple.' Better poems have been written. The soup is hot and her eyes water. Her mouth feels like a ravaged cavern and she feels the food sending a marker into her chest. A flag planted deep.

He looks away from her when one of the children cries. She notes his lips twitch: he usually shouts at them. He casts his eyes back at her.

'They your kids?' she asks.

'No, why?'

He has always lied to her face. They weren't meant to last more than a minute. A hot night, a dirty fusion, they were secretive. Then she let him tower over her. They once met in a street bar. The street bar closed. They stayed on the grubby metal chairs in the breeze block cubicle next to the gutter. Talking first, his arching talk, her spilling answers, until the city was quiet and he climbed over her and a baptism took place, water coursing from the bowels of somewhere, cheap beer fraying at the back of their throats. She now thinks these episodes were helpless and theatrical. She has had better lovers on clean beds. Men who didn't need an arena or the night's clawing.

She finds a hard rind in the soup and removes it from her mouth. *Wele.*

'You know I hate *wele* in the soup.'

He smiles. There was another game. She was Pig Meat. He was Bush Meat. She loved him because he had found what was common between them, he shone a light hard on her.

'You know,' he says. 'I can't believe I have you sitting here across from me. This is what I have always wanted.'

Sitting before her, flanked by palms scoring the punch-blue sky and the powdery wall behind him, there is no evidence of the wheelchair. He is a free man sitting there, free to wander to the railing and light a cigarette, lean over the rail showing off his shapely rump and long thighs, turning back to peruse her at the table. His hair is pulled back in his legendary, scruffy ponytail. His beard has grown long. He looks like a man in one of his own documentaries.

'So where shall I take you this afternoon? What would you like to see?'

She hasn't given any thought to what she would do here. She knows nothing about this country now. There is almost a week before them. Her throat tightens. He had called her only recently, eight months since the fall. Initially, he had been to the States for an operation. There had been a glimmer of hope, a keen doctor, cousin of a filmmaker friend. It hadn't worked. The soup sits in her stomach, a queasy burning. She flushes her throat with beer.

'I don't know.'

'Are you tired?'

'No, not at all.'

Perhaps she had expected him to be more miserable, more of a recluse, even ashamed of what had happened to him. Perhaps she was ashamed. She wasn't used to it yet.

'I want you to have a good time here.'

The young man drives them to the local beach. It is a trial to watch him parcelled into the car, the young man sweeping him from one seat to the other, one arm under his bottom, the other curved around his back. She watches him belt himself in. She sits in the back with a straw hat. She has changed into her swimming costume and now wears a sundress. Her arms feel flabby, her skin mottled. She is self-conscious. The dress is fairly long. She has brought flip-flops.

In the car, as they drive, she wants to cry and he turns around and sees her. She places her cheek on his shoulder and he cups her other cheek with his hand, which is cool. There is a snatch of his old smell between his fingers, deep where the skin forks apart. Her tears finish and she pulls away. He looks out the window. He has bundled his hair into a knitted cap.

Though the car park is full, his driver heads directly to the sandy entrance to the beach. She sees the water glittering, waves crashing, hears reggae from massive speakers. Helpers rush to the vehicle, standing in a circle when the driver lifts out the wheelchair, pulls the arms apart, placing a printed cushion on the seat sling. She sits there, watching him scoop up her old lover, arrange his trousered legs. She gets out. The crowd of hawkers and ragamuffins jostles around her, hands extended with peeled oranges, cinnamon gum, nail clippers. Ahead, the young man has tilted the chair and pulls him as a donkey with a cart. She looks at him and he is laughing at her grim face, telling her to get a move on.

They settle under a beach umbrella plugged into the sand outside one of the bars, a shack really. It is a busy afternoon but a table has somehow been freed for them. She senses he comes here a lot. With friends from the old days, not family members, the people he caroused with. Mostly men. She knows that the women who interested him all became lovers. Many would be weary of him now. She senses he also comes here alone and likes to strike up conversations, offering a beer to the coconut boy or a Danish pilot. She remembers his world views were almost sensual. He chiefly represented himself.

One of the young waitresses gives him a warm kiss on the cheek and his arm grasps her back, fingers in a star. She wonders if he can still have an erection. The girl is ripe and very dark.

They are served beers. The young driver has disappeared.

Later she sees him standing under an awning alone, sipping Fanta.

'Would you like a swim?'

'Not yet, not really.'

She doesn't want him to see her body. Before, they used to glide together. Hours were spent naked, examining each other's orifices, plunging until pain or fear or eclipse brought them back. Their intimacy has always haunted her. She wonders what he has done with other women.

'You're afraid I'll check out your bum?'

'Something like that.'

'Like to see mine?' He laughs. 'You know, I'm going to make love to you before you leave this place.'

She shakes her head slowly.

They would always have the blueprints for each other's bodies.

Before she is too drunk, she takes her towel down to the water's edge. She needs to pee and figures she'll do it in the sea. She wonders how long he will last after two beers. Maybe that is why the young man is waiting there. She doesn't know how it works yet. She takes off her dress and wades in, dunking herself in the water's cold clasp. Tropical, but the sea is always freezing. Ahead, the waves crash down and few people have gone out that far. She pees, a hot cloud on her leg. She was once caught in a rip here. Another time, a turd floated by her shoulder. She breaststrokes a little.

Refreshed, she walks back to where they were sitting, but his wheelchair is gone. She looks about. He can't have moved far. Then she sees the young man pulling hard, flicking up sand, the wheelchair tilted behind him. The chair is swung around and parked. She feels like embracing him, she knows the alcohol and drowsy sun are conspiring. She wonders if it is still illegal to go on the beach at night. They were encircled by soldiers once, down by one of the fancy hotels. The soldiers pulled down his trunks and played with him, laughing at his fine, spent cock.

The young man walks off to his shady spot under an awning. He stands there squinting at the surf.

'How was the water? I'd like to have a swim with you. In the morning could be good.'

When he called to tell her what had happened, he said he wanted to buy her a plane ticket. He said he had to see her. He asked her about dates. She could not speak. Eventually she told him some dates and was able to put off work and foster out her animals. It was a long, fretful trip, partly because he had rewired her all over again and she was back in his orbit. The keenest, most stringent thing she had ever done was to leave him. But he had spoken so plainly. She had never heard him speak so plainly.

She wipes the rim of the green bottle, chinks hers with his.

'Let's sit awhile,' he says.

The light softens after its bright peak. The day ends early here: it is dark by six o'clock. The sun seeps into her legs. She feels her skin tight and dry, wet behind the knees. Sand covers her shins. The chair is uncomfortable and she shifts from one buttock to the other. Her costume has dried quickly. She sees him looking at her arms. She covers her slight belly with her sarong. He has never worn sunglasses, his eyes have always stared at the world, even in the hottest places. She noticed reading glasses on the table at the house.

A hawker comes up to them with a tub on his head piled high with useless things. He stares at the man's headdress, then points to a shred of blue hair-netting that the girls use here when they scrub their skins. The seller has calves like yams and removes the contraption from his head, placing it on the sand and bringing forth socks, soap, chalk for ants. *Do they not want any of these fine tings*? But again, he points to the bright blue netting. He buys it with some greasy notes and gives it to her. It is a coarse blue spider web.

'A gift,' he says.

'Thank you.'

He calls behind him to the ripe waitress who comes out laughing, her tray flat on her hip. The young woman curls her arm around his neck and their faces are close. She used to feel so scalded when other women came up to him. But now she identifies this pulse, it feels innocuous. She looks away. The driver has stepped out from under the awning and is speaking on his mobile phone. People are beginning to trail back to the car park. A tiny girl with masses of beaded plaits wears sagging swimmers and sucks her thumb. Her mother has deep-blue tattoos sunken into her shoulders, one laced across her chest. Other people have just arrived. Two men in wide trousers and printed shirts, two girls with tidy hair. They set out a little way from the speakers then drop to the sand in a group. No hand-holding, no kisses. There are still religious people here, with staunch values.

The waitress leaves, her broad bare feet kick up sand as she sways. He has bought a Guinness for the hawker.

She glances at his beige trousers and the socks and canvas shoes someone has fitted onto his feet. He looks like a slim girl wearing cast-offs. He always wore jeans before. Jeans everywhere. Through deserts. Bare-chested in the house when she was drenched with heat. She tries to imagine him naked. His slack upper body tapering to the useless twins of his legs. She remembers taking him in her mouth, stroking his limbs. She remembers the weight of him, she can feel the different textures of him on her tongue.

'Perhaps we should go to the house now. I have a couple of things I have to do.'

He says this as though he has forgotten an appointment. The young man comes over, manoeuvring him through the parade of people headed home. Their vehicle is at the head of the car park and again she watches painfully as his body is transferred. She will have to get used to this. He looks tired. On the way home he does not speak and she feels as though it was a mistake to have come here. He stares over the neighbourhoods. At the house, his chair is smacked apart again and his body is lifted and he is wheeled to the stairs. The young man carries him up into the house.

She steps out of the car into the yard. Children and mistresses have gone someplace else and she smells smoke from a charcoal cooker. The walls of the house are brown with grime and the palm trees are pushed deep into the dirt before the back fence. She walks over and touches one. Looks up to the clutch of coconuts at the top, genitals under a skirt. It's been a while since she's had sex. She supposes he can see it on her. She walks over to the next tree and flattens her hands around it, feeling the dry ridges and ruts. She remembers how he made her lie on the rooftop and describe clouds, a thing she'd hadn't done since she was a kid. It never rang true – she knew his childhood had been stolen – his delight in unmarred things.

She still doesn't know what she should ask him. Why she is even here. She looks up, imagining he is leaning bare-chested over the railing, smoking, looking rangy, hungry for her. She hears a sound from the shower block at the back. A toilet is flushed and a squat, messy-looking woman walks out and back into the house, wiping her hands on her shift.

Upstairs, the door to his bedroom is closed and she hears water running. She wants to shower but doesn't know if there is enough pressure for two of them to run at the same time. She leaves her things in the spare room, goes out onto the veranda and rubs the sand from her shins with a towel. She is still wearing her swimming costume. She can smell food cooking downstairs in the kitchen. He has always had mediocre, cranky cooks who would leave after big fights with everybody, usually involving theft. She doesn't care for food right now and doubts she will this evening. On the table there is a carafe of water and two glasses, one with droplets inside. She drinks.

There is still no sound from his bedroom. She knew there would be a lot of dead time here, when he would rest or have other things to do. She has brought work with her, but she doesn't feel much like it. She sits outside drinking water. The neighbourhood is quiet. They were all stylish homes once.

The young man comes out of the bedroom and closes the door. It's hard to read his face. It is as though he embodies what has happened, even more than the paralysed man in the room, and when he leaves he takes away slabs of the tragedy. She is glad he is remote. She would not have liked some chatty nurse. She hears a voice from the bedroom. It is a clean, clear voice that projects and rises. She realises she checks her face in the mirror.

'I'm sorry, I had a bit of a spell there. I'm not supposed to drink alcohol.'

She thought as much.

'I needed it, you know. Your fault.'

She looks about the room, sees a photo of herself. There are photos of other people too, some of whom she remembers. She sees him next to a tall young woman with a broad forehead, the image of him. A pixie child with dreadlocks. She looks back to the photograph of herself. Her hair used to reach her buttocks and he would dress her in it.

'I'm happy to have you in here again.'

He has showered and wears a different shirt. He wears printed drawstring trousers and looks more like himself. His hair is pulled back and his beard looks combed. The young man has placed him in a wider wheelchair by the window. His feet are bare. He sees her looking at them, watches the journey of her eyes.

'Come here.'

She shakes her head.

'You're not afraid of a little guy in a wheelchair?'

Now she wants to know what happened. Why he was up a ladder. Why *him* when there are idle young men on every street corner here, all of them more able than a sixty-year-old filmmaker.

It's not the first time he's read her thoughts.

'I was stupid. Very stupid. I was checking the phone cable. It was worn through, the wires were exposed. I wasn't getting an Internet signal. Couldn't get a technician to get over here. You know how it is. I fell onto the cement ledge you can see down there. Didn't feel a thing. Just flying. Descent. And a crack inside. A horrible crack. They did their best, you know.'

She worked out that it must have happened in February.

The heaviest time of the year for her. Winter. Her favourite dog put down. And, over here, a spinal cord severed. *This.*

'I wanted to call you. I wanted to hear your voice. I waited because I thought there was a chance. Now I know there is no chance.'

She wonders who walked him through it, who was there when he woke up. A wife? A daughter? A sturdy old friend or half-brother? She doesn't know what the fuck she is doing here. And yet she knows, she knows.

'I'd like to swim with you. Shall we go for a swim together tomorrow?'

She nods.

Neither of them are hungry that evening. She finds a tin of tea leaves next to the kettle on a small refrigerator in the corner of the living room. She makes two mugs of tea and wheels him onto the veranda.

In the night she hears his door open and close quietly. She hears murmuring. She can't get back to sleep. The hot food completes its course through her and she sits on the loo listening to mosquitoes whining. She scratches bites on her legs. She drinks more water, feeling cramps in her stomach. It is dark in the room though there is a violet fluorescent light on outside somewhere below. There are bars on her window. She lies down again. The sea is inaudible, only the palm leaves stroke each other. She wonders if he is listening to the same thing, if the nights have become a dark tunnel. Or if there is a woman from downstairs spreading warmth through his body, pushing its force against the border where his nerves dissolve.

At daybreak he is dressed and showered, wheeled onto the veranda, waiting for her. He looks happy. He motions for her to come over and she feels bedraggled, creased and puffy. He tugs down her arm and kisses her cheek, which feels loose against the bone. His lips are warm, she knows their deep pressure. She feels a little spring, a fountain. She pulls away, closes her cardigan around her. The damp morning surrounds them. She never rises this early.

She knows what will happen. Somehow, she will lift him onto the bed. She does not know how their clothes will be removed, but they will be removed. He will cup his upper body to her back, a hand across her breasts, hooked under her shoulder. She will haul his knees behind her knees and her feet will enclose his lifeless feet. Later, she will trace the rim around his body, the fault line, the front. She will bring her wet cheek to the neat laceration on his spine.

It begins to rain. They both watch the morning shower, a clean curtain.

6.
We Will Dance in Lampedusa
Stanley Kenani

'What is the first thing we'll do when we arrive?' Bibiana says to me.

'We'll make love,' I say. 'Right there on the beach at Lampedusa.'

She glances at the others and lowers her voice. 'How can you say such a thing?'

'They don't understand our language. They speak Amharic, Somali, Tigrigna, Oromo . . . They don't know what we're talking about.'

'They say we'll arrive in twenty-four hours, no? My days are not good.'

'What do you mean, "My days are not good"?'

'Come on, you know what I'm talking about. We can't risk it.'

'Okay, in that case we'll dance. We'll hug and kiss and dance.'

'Yes, we'll dance,' says Bibiana.

We both laugh and everyone in the boat stares at us. A baby begins to cry as though protesting that anyone could have the nerve to laugh in circumstances so dire. I turn to gaze at receding Tripoli: at the towering buildings some of which have been ruined by the savage blows of bombs; at the minarets from which the muezzin's call above the gunfire still reaches us at sea like a radio at low volume; and at the beaches with white polished pebbles not yet stained by the bloody war.

The boat rocks from side to side. The symphony of waves is pleasant to my ears. In a flash, I drop my hand from around Bibiana's waist to grip the boat's edge. It is frighteningly audacious that they have managed to pack all of us in here. It is a small boat, like a plastic dinghy. I don't know how many we are – around seventy – in a boat designed to carry less than half that number. But I hear it can be worse on trips like these, so I suppose I should not be too concerned about the headcount. Thank heavens the boat is in good shape, its engine purring powerfully as we move with ease towards our destination. What a blessing that Bibiana and I are here, heading for this most precious of places. It's a miracle, really, given how impossible it all seemed before we set off from home.

I turn again to look back to where we have come from. Africa is receding into our past. Tripoli is getting smaller. We can no longer hear the sound of the city's bombs and gunfire and its call for prayer has now been muted by distance. Goodbye, Libya. I will never forget you.

★

Entering Tripoli was like walking into a blazing furnace.

'Courage,' Abdul-Jabaar kept telling us, 'you have to have courage. I'll leave you with Moustafa al-Arab, a close friend. You'll be safe. The boat people will come for you when the weather is right.'

With those words he left us, after having taken us on the most perilous journey from our home city of Lilongwe on the southern part of our continent, after driving us in trucks disguised as fuel tankers, after crossing crocodile-infested rivers with us on shaky canoes, after making us pay double the amount we had initially agreed on so he could bribe immigration officials at numerous borders, after getting nearly roasted by the heat of the Sahara Desert, after surviving on only biscuits and water, sometimes for weeks, after fending off bandits who attacked us in the middle of the desert. After all that, Abdul-Jabaar left us in the hands of another stranger, in a Tripoli that had been set on fire by people who wanted their country to give them either freedom or death.

If Moustafa al-Arab had not hidden us in a garage at his Souq al Juma'ah house for three weeks, we probably would have perished. The fight to topple the dictator had turned bloody, and we came at a time when the fire was just beginning to burn too hot. For three weeks, we endured the sounds of guns and earth-shattering bombs. When we peered into the street through the crack in the wall, cars roamed in all directions, menacing weapons mounted behind them, their drivers looking for humanity to mow down. Sometimes we saw people, probably immigrants from our part of the world, being shot in cold blood. Moustafa told us that all those we saw killed, including women and children, were mercenaries hired by the dictator to fight the rebels.

Bombs seemed to fall from the heavens as though an amateur player of a video war game was pressing the wrong buttons. Twice, the bombs fell unpleasantly close, and shrapnel gave our garage a good shaking, eliciting cries of 'Allahu Akbar' from those hiding with us. For three weeks, we saw no sunshine except through the crack in the wall. It was always heads or tails whether we would be alive the next minute. At the sound of every bomb, my stomach turned, and I nearly let loose in my trousers on many occasions. Bombs are fun in the war movies, but not when they are raining on the buildings across the street. I don't remember hearing anybody laugh during those three weeks. We did not taste a moment of peace.

Where did these others hide? At Moustafa al-Arab's there was only Bibiana and me and seven other guys. He fed us bread and tea. Morning, noon and night, bread and tea, for three weeks. That was what he could afford, he said. The only thing that changed was the type of bread: hard-crusted bread, soft bread, normal-looking bread, or bread that was long and thin, like a policeman's baton. Sometimes I wondered whether, in a moment of despair, he might turn us in. It would be an easy thing for him because there was no difference in appearance between the mercenaries and us; but he seemed to be a good man.

Now, as the boat's engine purrs with a reassuring steadiness, I am happy we're still alive after the worst three weeks of our lives. I never want to return to that place. Goodbye, Africa. God willing, we'll see each other again only through Google Earth.

★

The sea is calm and accommodating, like a patient hostess. The boat people must be geniuses for choosing a time so apt for our travel. Everyone in the boat is silent, perhaps thinking

97

of the paradise that lies at the end of our journey. The only
sound is of the engine, as the boat ploughs the water apart,
heading north. We are far from everything now. All around
us there is nothing but water. The fear in me becomes too
severe when I let my eyes stretch to the horizon, so I sometimes close them to think only of better things. I have never
been in the middle of so much water before. Abdul-Jabaar
was right: you have to have a lot of courage to successfully
leave your country, your people and your continent.

'The journey is not an easy one,' he'd said as he smoked
his cigarette in a small, dingy restaurant in Lilongwe's Devil
Street about a year ago.

I did not know that by courage he meant being ready to
be in a situation such as this, floating in the middle of a vast,
deep ocean to which our boat must seem like a lost beach
ball that has strayed too far from the shore.

Bibiana grips my hand. 'I'm afraid,' she says.

'Don't be,' I say, hoping that my voice has not betrayed
my own fear. 'There are only nineteen hours to go.
Nineteen. After that we'll be in Lampedusa.'

Bibiana is shivering. 'But what if …?'

'Don't let such thoughts disturb you, my love. We'll be
fine. Trust me.'

Bibiana, amazing as ever, has always been in my life, or I
have always been in hers. As far back as my memory
stretches, to when I was about five years old – even then,
she was there, playing with me in the rain, our mothers running after us, shouting, 'Come in, you two, you'll catch
fever!' after which they would grab us and take us for a bath
as we giggled. I can say we grew up as lovers, so that when
we finally got down to kissing and making love, our bodies

responded in such an energetic way that it was clear this was the moment we had always waited for.

All the twenty-seven years of our existence were filled with memories so vivid that time was powerless to erase them. Our parents were the best of friends in the neighbourhood of Lilongwe where we lived. As I was born first, I would wait for a week to celebrate our birthdays together, through the years of our kindergarten, through primary school where we shared a desk, until after secondary school, when our paths split. I went to the School of Humanities, while she opted for the National College of Nursing. By that time we had already made love, but at her insistence we agreed to slow down to prevent a ruinous pregnancy that could have stalled her progress towards a college degree. And then, a year into our studies, we both lost our parents. The car they were travelling in from their holiday upcountry collided with a bus.

When I graduated from college, as I looked for a job, Bibiana asked me to move in with her. Though her salary was too low to support two adults, she insisted on accommodating me. She was incredibly generous and went so far as sparing the little she had to take us out for dinner once in a while, or to visit Lake Malawi, where we would lie on velvet-soft beaches of white sand, or swim in water that was clear and blue like the sky above it.

It was at that time that I began to feel my country spitting me out. Our government, the biggest employer of graduates with my kind of qualification, had suddenly decided that humanities were no longer important. They had stopped recruiting secondary-school teachers with qualifications in this field, and would be making these subjects optional, effectively phasing them out. The humanities had been judged irrelevant and downgraded. We were going to be a science-only nation. This, our minister of education said, would put our country firmly on the path to development: 'With proper roots in science, we can send one of our own sons into space within twenty years.'

After three years of job hunting, I had had enough. I needed to leave the country. Three of my former classmates from college had gone to Ireland, where it was clear they were prospering. We saw their photos on Facebook, wearing expensive suits, smiling as though they had just been crowned masters of the universe. We saw them disembarking from limousines or dancing at parties. We saw them drinking in bars or celebrating birthdays with huge cakes and lots of wine. I too wanted to be there, to be happy.

I had to move. Initially, I wanted to go to the United Kingdom. But when I went to the High Commission to apply for a visa, they wanted a letter from an employer I did not have. They wanted payslips for my last three months of employment, and half a year of bank statements. They demanded that I submit a copy of a letter from the person or institution inviting me to the UK, complete with the address where I would be residing. The cash I would be bringing along too – how much would it be? As though they had not asked for too much already, they insisted on collecting my fingerprints, the way our authorities do with criminals. How, I wondered, did people ever manage to go abroad?

It was at that time I learnt of the skills of Abdul-Jabaar, he who could take you anywhere in the world without a visa. Through a friend of a friend, I arranged to meet him in Devil Street. A man with bushy eyebrows and a perpetual frown, he got straight to the point. All I needed was $2,000 for him to take me to the Mediterranean, and then $1,000 for his colleagues to take me by boat to the other side. To avoid any misunderstanding, he stressed that the dollars had to be American.

Although I had no idea where to get the money, I decided we should do it. I told Bibiana: 'Finally, we have a realistic chance of moving to Europe. There's a man who can take us to Lampedusa. After that, we're on our own. All I need now is to raise the money for the trip.'

'Drop that idea,' she said. 'Stay. Something good will come your way soon. Have patience, please.'

'Patience? Three years of job-hunting is not enough patience for you?'

'It is, but just a little more.'

'For how long? Until my hair is grey and my back bent by age? No, I can't wait that long. We need to leave now.'

It took us weeks of arguing. At one point, we did not talk to each other for days. Still, I stood my ground. Then she tried to change her approach, telling me harrowing tales of how some had been deported from Europe with nothing, or how they had ended up begging or sleeping in the streets. I countered with stories of those who returned with lots of money, or those who sought asylum and got the right papers and jobs.

'As far as I know,' she said, 'asylum is only granted to those running away from war.'

'Is poverty peace then?' I asked.

When it was clear she had given up her opposition, I moved to part two of the grand plan, which was logistics. How would I raise the money for the journey?

The answer, finally, came to me in a way I could never have imagined. An opportunity suddenly presented itself for me to sell my kidney to a Very Important Person whose name I was asked never to disclose to anyone. It was something I stumbled upon by chance. Somebody who had attempted to donate a kidney was ruing his missed luck in my presence at a local pub. Apparently, he had been turned away because he belonged to the wrong blood group. At once, I saw my opportunity and decided to grab it without hesitation.

After I bought the fellow three beers, he loosened up and gave further crucial details. The man looking for the donation was a top politician who did not want his chances of re-election ruined by doubts about his health. He was prepared to pay well. Scores of potential donors, I was told, had tried without success. The doctors carried out so many tests – for hepatitis, tuberculosis, gonorrhoea, syphilis and a lot more. They checked potential donors' HIV statuses. Though I was apprehensive about all these requirements, when I went through the tests I came out clean. The doctor who counselled me in preparation for the donation remarked, 'You are in remarkably good health.'

Finally, when all the testing was over, I informed Bibiana.

'You are frightening me,' she said. 'Please don't do this.'

'I must,' I said.

'Can't you see you'll die?'

'It's entirely harmless, Bibiana.'

'There's a reason our bodies must have two kidneys.'

'Scientists have found it harmless to share kidneys, Bibiana.'

We were about to have our dinner that evening. She left the table and did not return. After the meal, I followed her to the bedroom. I lay next to her and tried to put my arm around her. She pushed it off and faced away from me.

'Listen, my love,' I said, 'I've not killed anyone. I've not robbed anyone. It's my kidney I'm selling. Can't you understand?'

She did not respond.

Eventually, we agreed to disagree. I donated the kidney and went through a period of recovery for a couple of months. This was one of the many times when Bibiana showed how much she truly cared about me. Despite her opposition to the idea, she was very supportive when the deed was finally done. She took leave from work to be by my side. There wasn't any serious harm done to my body. I just felt tired for the first week or two and was unable to lift heavy items for a few more weeks after that. Eventually, I regained my strength, and felt ready for the long trip. But when all was set, Bibiana's doubts returned.

'Now that you have all this money, why not just start some kind of business?' she suggested.

'You think a business starts just like that?' I snapped. 'You have to have an idea, a plan. You must possess the right skills. It's not just because you have money in your hands.'

I realised that my tone had been excessively harsh, for she looked pained, so I walked over to where she stood and put my hand on her shoulder.

'I'm sorry,' I said. 'It's just that we can't change our plans now. My mind is not here anymore. I feel this country has rejected me. We have to leave, my love.'

I kissed her, but she did not respond.

Her mood soon brightened, however, and she began to speak a lot about our future in Lampedusa. This was after matters were fast-tracked for us in a surprising way. A month before our departure, Abdul-Jabaar warned that we risked being separated along the way if we did not have a marriage certificate. There might be a need to prove to immigration authorities of some countries that we were travelling as a family. So we quickly arranged to exchange vows before the Registrar of Marriages, Births and Deaths.

'We'll have a proper church ceremony in Lampedusa,' I promised her.

★

Now here we are, in this boat, heading towards our future in the company of strangers.

'Don't be afraid,' I try to reassure her. 'We've come a long way. Only a few more hours to go, my love. Only a few more hours.' My arm circling her waist, I say: 'Close your eyes if you can't stand the sea. Think of the beauty of Lampedusa, where you'll be working as a nurse, where your monthly salary will be more than your annual salary back home. Think of the house we'll be living in. Think of only good things and you'll be fine.'

She closes her eyes. The shivering has subsided now. I hold her tighter, her head resting on my shoulder. We're almost there.

★

Less than ten hours to our destination and, oh God, the engine has stopped. Several hours after I managed to calm Bibiana's nerves, without warning, the engine died.

I look around. There's not a glimpse of land for a determined survivor to swim to. Water everywhere, up to the horizon in every direction. The captain looks at us. We look at each other, all of us, without a word. Bibiana's grip on my hand tightens.

'What's happening, Captain?' I ask.

He, however, speaks a language I do not know. He tries to explain, but I understand nothing. Some, it seems, have understood, because they speak among themselves, their voices rising in panic. Others begin to cry.

'What's going on?' Bibiana asks me.

'I don't know.' I say. 'It seems we have engine trouble.'

'Oh God!' she screams.

'Everything will be all right,' I try to calm her. I wish I could believe these words myself.

The captain tries to start the engine again. It sputters and dies, sputters and dies, again and again. He shakes his head, sweating. He speaks. From the gestures of his hands and the gentleness of his voice, I think he is saying everything is going to be all right. It had better be. Everyone around me is crying.

I know that help will come from somewhere. I have seen ships along the way. I am certain that someone will soon spot us and rescue us. For the first time in years, I utter the novena of St Jude.

'Most holy apostle, St Jude, pray for us . . .'

★

Now the situation has degenerated into our worst fears. The sea has suddenly changed its attitude. It is no longer calm. It is treating us like unwelcome visitors, as if we have invaded its space. What began as welcome rain has turned into a violent storm. Mountains of water are flinging us up and down with force so great that about fifteen people were thrown overboard the first time a wave hit us. Everyone around me is wailing. Even as I think these thoughts, there is another torrent of water coming. And we, like the rest of the sea's debris, are going in any direction the wind wants to take us. I have lost a sense of east or west, north or south. I am cold and hungry.

'Water!' Bibiana demands. 'I need water.'

'Water!' I call out, my feeble voice battling the raging wind. 'Does anyone have some water?'

★

Another wave comes with great speed, like a hungry shark. We can do nothing but shriek. It swallows us and tosses us and suffocates us and shakes us, and I am gripping the edge of the boat with all my strength. I cannot breathe, I cannot see, the force is too strong and overpowering. And then suddenly it is gone, and I am gasping. I can now see that the sun has risen. The boat is full of water. The others are using their hands and anything else they can to drain the water, or else we will sink. Bibiana is here, coughing and gasping at once. The boat is emptier, as many more have been sucked in by the deep and hungry sea – men, women, babies.

'Most holy apostle, St Jude,' I beg, 'please do not abandon us . . .'

★

A helicopter! Oh, St Jude, thank you, thank you! First it passed us, but now it has circled back. Our captain is waving at it. We all join in, waving. It's flying low now, and some people are peering out from it. We wave more, crying and begging, 'Please help! Help!' and they are taking photographs, it seems. That black thing pointing at us, isn't it a camera? A baby begins to cry, the kind of cry that can only be silenced with food. Maybe they have something they could throw down to us? A bottle of water, perhaps? Or a tin of biscuits? The woman lifts the baby with both hands and waves it at them.

'We die of thirst!' I shout, pointing at the baby.

But with the helicopter's heavy engine sound and the whirl of the rotating blades above it, I doubt they have heard me. The helicopter circles around us once, then gathers speed and leaves us. We gaze at it as it becomes smaller and smaller until it cannot be seen any more.

'I think,' I say to Bibiana, 'they'll send boats to rescue us. Lampedusa can't be far now. The sea must have tossed us close to the shore.'

'You think so?' She is not convinced.

'Yes, we'll soon be rescued.'

The wait begins. The sea is calm now. The sky is cloudless. It has become warm. Too warm. The heat is beginning to sear our skin. I hope the helicopter people will bring help fast. The hunger is so severe I could eat a raw fish if I got hold of one. Helicopter, please come back.

'Most holy apostle, St Jude, pray for us. We are hopeless and alone.'

★

It is day three.

The helicopter has yet to return. Unable to stand the

thirst, Bibiana has been drinking sea water, despite my advice not to. It has made her sick. The waves came back last night and took more lives, including the captain's. We're completely lost. The sea is calm again, but this is of little comfort if help does not come.

★

I can't count the hours or the days any more. I have lost track of day and night. I am weak, unable to sit up. From time to time I raise my head to look around, to confirm that I am still alive. We're still drifting like those little paper boats Bibiana and I used to throw in the rainwater that formed rivulets next to the veranda of my parents' house. I make an effort to confirm that Bibiana is also alive. Yes, she's still lying here next to me, her weak hand curled around my backside.

'Water,' she whispers. She wants to drink more sea water.

'It is the sea water that is making you vomit,' I croak. I try to run a tongue on my dry and heavily-cracked lips, but the saliva does not come. It's as though a fire is burning in my throat.

'Water.' Bibiana is desperate. 'I need water.'

A man stands up all too suddenly, limps to the edge of the boat and plunges himself into the sea like a tree felled by stormy winds.

Another man, to my right, has taken off his clothes. He is twisting his pubic hair into nasty dreadlocks, howling like a dog.

I close my eyes.

'Oh most glorious apostle, St Jude, we implore you. Bring visible and speedy help.'

★

I don't know how many days we've been at sea, but somehow we're still alive. Our boat is still floating, with just few of us lying in it, some face up, others face down, a couple sideways, their bodies curled into question marks. Bibiana cannot move, but I can feel her heart beating. She and I and about five others, including a toddler, are the only souls left clinging to life.

All my strength is gone. Still, I manage to raise my head, and behold, buildings! There are buildings in front of me! Looking upwards, I see signs of life. Carrion birds are hovering over us, waiting for us to die. Sorry, birds. You'll not eat today. We're in Lampedusa now, a few hundred metres from the city. They'll come and rescue us.

'Bibiana,' I say, shaking her with renewed strength. 'Bibiana! Wake up! We've reached the shores of Lampedusa. Wake up!'

Sounds of approaching engines. Men jumping on board. A babble of voices. Hands lifting me up. I feel a shadow of darkness passing over me. Who are these people? St Jude, save me! Please, most glorious apostle, save me!

★

Time has passed that I cannot account for. I have just opened my eyes to find myself lying in bed. I can see Bibiana in the bed next to mine, intravenous bags dangling above her, attached to some kind of stand. I want to speak to her but my voice will not come. She is trying to say something, but what comes from her mouth is only two words, over and over: 'The sea . . . the sea . . .'

I am breathing with the help of a machine. I feel as

though a vacuum cleaner has been inserted into my nose. I can see two small bags of intravenous fluid hanging over me as well. I want to move my hand, but a nurse appears from nowhere and pins it down, muttering something that at first I fail to understand. She looks at me and smiles.

'*Allahu Akbar*,' she says. '*Allahu Akbar. Bismi-llahi r-rahmani r-rahim . . .*'

Allah is great. In the name of Allah, the Merciful, the Compassionate . . . My understanding of her Arabic stops there. Through hazy eyes, I can see the writing on her badge. It reads: 'Amina Hussein. Metiga Military Hospital. Tripoli', followed by some Arabic writing.

This cannot be true. We left Libya many days ago. We must be in Lampedusa. We must be on the island, on whose beaches Bibiana and I will soon dance. Perhaps I am still unconscious, or having a bad dream. When I wake up the nurse's badge will read 'Ospedale Santo Spirito', or something like that. Bibiana will work as a nurse. I will get a job. They must have a job for me. I can teach the *Divine Comedy. Inferno, Purgatorio, Paradiso*, I can teach all that stuff.

7.
At the Mouth of the River
Barry Reddin

The calm,
Cool face of the water
Asked me for a kiss.

—Langston Hughes
'Suicide's Note'

I.

Brussels has some unique features. It has a mishmash face, a face that maybe could have done with either a little more or a little less World War II and, yes, the people are a bit mishmash as well but, and stay with me here, where Brussels really stands out is in its odour. That smell that permeates life between the concrete and steel and glass rows of a city. When you turn a corner on a summer's day, when the air is fragrant with the bloom of city trees and the humidity of life entangled and pulsating and living and, suddenly, your olfactory senses are assailed by civilisation. That queer funk that only the human body can produce. The smell of sweat and sex and hair product. Every city has its own unique combinations. In the case of Brussels you are routinely assaulted at the gaping mouths of metro stations, those cavernous gateways to transitory perdition, by a smell that is both enticingly sweet and simultaneously foul. The smell of waffles and piss. It's everywhere on a hot midsummer day. On Avenue Louise, Boulevard Anspach, Toison D'Or. Everywhere. If you live in a city you grow to love its *parfum*, its cologne, its inimitable body odour. If you love a city, as I do, you can't imagine a moment without it. The busy high notes of fragrant coffees and pastries and car exhaust, the base low notes of dog shit. I love my city. I love cities. The noise, the humidity, the confrontations and conflicts of people and colour and choice. So imagine my horror when I am forced to leave for the cooler and more expansive climes of Scandinavia.

I rush through the concourse of Zaventem Airport loaded with luggage and panic and sweat because of my job. I do not hold down a nine-to-five, and I offer thanks everyday for this sweet miracle, but I do have to work to tight schedules and, as in the case this morning, I am often at the mercy of Federal Express. For, you see, I am a book reviewer. I can hear the wheels in your head turning already, *How can that be stressful? How can that make you late*? Well, since I assume you are asking, I write a biweekly column for a major literary review in London, I contribute to two monthly publications in New York and Los Angeles and I also have my very own blog and Twitter account to maintain. It is a lot to cover and often I am left waiting for a piece of literature to arrive for my dissection. So here I am, having left my oversized luggage at the baggage drop, and I have moved through the security check with relative ease. The joys of late afternoon flying are not to be overstated, if only because of the lack of queuing. I find a nice little perch close to my gate and await the 16.50 Finnair flight to Helsinki.

The book I am reviewing is the third volume of Professor Peter Michelson's Imperial America series, grotesquely and portentously titled *Camelot: An Unfinished Dream*. Just what the world needs: another insipid celebration of the gaudiness and the glamour of the VD president and his over-hyped, over-blown, over-sexed family.

I lumber onto the plane once called. No matter how many times I travel I am always quietly incensed by the glares of the air hostesses as I board the plane. Yes, they smile and welcome me aboard, but the up-and-down they give me is emasculating. I am big – round, to be precise. I have a relatively pallid complexion and my cut, be it on my head or the general state of my jib, is not what it should be. I am aware of this and I can attest that the myth of the jolly fat man is exactly that. I take my seat: business class, though on this flight the only separation is a finely embroidered curtain that partially disrupts the gaze of those behind. I fire up my laptop once informed that I may, and begin the simple task of putting my criticisms down, but today it is not coming easy. My mind is easily distracted by the offer of coffee, water or juice, by the complimentary copy of the *Financial Times*, by the shrinking view of my city and my civilisation below. I write best with the bustle of car horns and revved engines, and the quiet tintinnabulations of a city.

The woman next to me, her name escapes me now, initiates a conversation without my assistance, but with the expressed necessity of my involvement, about how much she loved her first trip to Brussels. I smile, nod and mmm-hmm in the right places, but her inane chatter gives me a throbbing toothache. Everything rendered in mind-numbingly broken English and covering such topics as the divergent weather personalities of Belgium and Finland, Tove Jansson's Moomin characters and the size and temperament of the Finnish mosquito. I couldn't even enjoy my in-flight meal: reindeer mayonnaise salad on rye bread. The flight was made bearable by the landing however. The approach brought us into view of a fiery red sun burning hard and unforgiving over the spruce and pines below. The plane touches down smoothly, and I make my escape with smiles and safe-trip-homes. I fight the impulse to say, 'Until next time', for fear that the universe might accept this as a challenge.

Sadly, my journey has not come to an end. I have a ten-hour wait ahead of me at the Helsinki Airport, the local Hilton being fully booked, and I not up to traipsing into the city in search of a bed.

Now, usually, I would find the nearest spirit purveyor and order up a nightcap but, sadly, things have not been working out for me in that department of late. Many rages and stupors and blackouts have left my body, my soul and my marriage in tatters. The romantic ideal of the scribbler's life is anything but. I can handle the rotten dysentery after-taste in the morning. I can accept the lapses in recall, the trepidation and shame of not knowing what I said the night before and to whom I said it, and I can live with the pene-trating construction work that wakes me right behind the eyes of a morning, the searing drops of solder dripping onto my frontal lobe with every loud noise or careless whisper. All of this I can do. What I can't do, the element that wore me down and made me see the light, to bandy about a few clichés, was the look of horror and anger and frustration and disappointment on my wife's face each time I subjected myself to a binge. I always offered up a pitiful 'Never again', but, eventually, she said 'Enough'. My credit was worthless. The words coming out of my mouth were just useless and empty sounds, with no meaning attached. So I became sober. That is, I abstain from alcohol and I have also tried to keep the caffeine intake to a minimum.

This is not easy when much of my travel time is associated with drinking at airports while enjoying the clippings of other people's conversations, but I park myself in a leather booth at the airport's Café Tori, the abating shades of indigo in the evening sky embracing the red-orange sun, and begin reading and note-making on Professor Michelson's *disasterpiece.*

> . . . since the young president was shot dead at the tender age of forty-six, it is self-evident that his life was "unfinished", and, if you choose to assume the younger attorney general, by the time of his essential anointing, was a foregone conclusion as the bearer of the New Frontier torch when assassinated so coolly in a Californian hotel kitchen, then I suppose it is safe to assume that the dream was indeed *unfinished.*

Concentration is difficult with the din of the twenty-four-hour news cycle playing somewhere nearby. The usual celebration of carnage and human greed sang in the clipped resonance of Suomi, an inaccessible language I will one day have to call my own. If I haven't mentioned it yet, my wife is Finnish.

Sleep does not come easily at an airport and has to be

snatched and held like a lover who is too quick to wander. The benches are at least leather, but the slight decline between seat and back leaves one lying in a semi-paralytic state after a short while. If fellow suffering refugees don't wake you with their zombie shuffling, then the natural panic of a numb limb will. The subsequent vibrato of pins and needles will keep you awake and, before you know it, you will be back in the Tori Café. Sunrises are deceptive in midsummer here. The sun begins its skyward saunter at 3.30 AM and is in full gallop by 8.00. My morning begins with a mind-quickening non-alcoholic Lapin Kulta beer (read: reindeer piss), followed by the airport greatest hits of stale croissant and weak over-priced coffee. Breakfast of champions.

I make my way to the gate for my connecting flight to Joensuu, a university town perched on the mouth of the Pielisjoki River as it rolls into Lake Saimaa. I feel stale, and I long for the concrete jungle I have left behind.

I pick up a copy of the in-flight travel magazine to read a little about my intended destination. Joensuu literally means 'the mouth of the river'. It was founded in 1848 by Tsar Nicholas I and is often referred to as the forest capital of Europe. Super.

The view as we land is inspiring: pine and birch forests marching unchecked toward the horizon, with only pristine lakes to disrupt the uniformity. The plane touches down and I quickly remove my hand luggage from overhead and step out into blazing heat. The crisp air of my fantasies has been replaced with some Goya-esque Iberian nightmare. The breeze is a not-too-distant cousin of the whirling current that greets you when you open a fan-assisted oven to check on a casserole. I choke it in and tread quickly to the terminal. It's a small collection of bricks and mortar, provincial. Off-white walls, purple upholstery, grey uniforms and faces. There isn't even a divide between arrivals and departures. So much for rigorous security. The single luggage belt creaks to life after a sweaty and uncomfortable eternity in the low air-con cattle shed, and I am delighted to quickly grasp my bag and run. I miss the artificially cooled sophistication of my city life, of a cool bar and my laptop and my reviewing.

Outside, I wheel my grey, hard-sided ogre of a suitcase toward the airline's bus, a small shuttle with a friendly driver who smiles and nods me along when I say 'to university'. I climb aboard and, within minutes, we are breezing through the countryside. Flashes of sunlight between the heavy forest walls create a disconcerting strobe effect, and I am forced to look at my feet for a time. The countryside is already trying to kill me. How do people live in the wilds like this? My wife is a native of the green and peasant land (that's not a mistype). She was raised among the hill-billy dreams of reindeer farms and forests and endless winters. Of heaving axes and cleaving wood. Of beards and flannel. What on earth does she see in me? Fat and cerebral and nearly always carrying a layer of permasweat. I make her laugh though. Or, at least, I did at first. We'd go out together, and I'd be witty and humorous and we'd fall into bed entwined and enraptured. She always wanted to be by my side. She encouraged me to grow a beard and let my hair grow a bit and, yes, maybe it does suit me more but I would never tell her that. Sadly, my charms have begun to wane of late and, nowadays, I'm mundane and irritable and unsmiling. An amoeba of bitter critiques and back-handed comments and stale beer breath.

My wife had headed north a month ago, ostensibly for work, but with a friend's wedding tied into the bargain. Hence my tardy arrival. I am armed with my own meagre few wedding-worthy clothes, of course, but this hard-sided suitcase also contains the all-important dress that my beloved will don; she will shame all others.

I am a little concerned when we come to a stop and the driver phonetically pronounces 'oo-nee-vur-city'. I step out into the unknown and, as the bus bleeds away into the light morning traffic, I struggle into the university's quad to find shelter. Sadly, the unique design of this campus prevents any protection from the early morning sun, so I stand at the mercy of a lost Mediterranean orb while trying to call my beloved. 'Oh-ate-nyan-won . . . is not available to take your call, so please leave a message . . . BEEP.' The sky is a fault-less azure pane through which the intense glare of a malevolent deity has its cruel gaze fixed upon me. 'Fower-seecks-ate . . . is not available to take your call so please leave a message . . . BEEP.' The gaze is pitiless and judgemental and asks questions. *Who are you? What are you doing here?* '. . . is not available to take your call so please leave a message . . . BEEP.'

The mean and brutal immortal taunts me. *You are alone in my land?* The air is still and the traffic has ceased. I am unsettled by the silence. Silence is not golden, it is dark and threatening. Give me the discarded symphony of traffic any day. I stand squinting into the distance, praying for the image of my significant other to emerge from the shimmering horizon beyond. Those familiar bars to the Grande

Valse begin ringing in my pocket, and I pull my Nokia (what else?) out and breathe a heavy sigh of relief as I see my wife's name on the screen. I answer. She apologises and is surprised I am here already. She's close by, so I hang tight and wait. Sure enough, she whirls along on her rental bike and is a monument to *beauté* in a white summer dress with oxblood bows, her flowing cinnamon hair trailing behind and sweeping forward as she brakes, framing her amiable face. Her coral lips ever smiling, and her eyes wicked and teasing, the green of an outraged sea. She leans forward and plants a kiss on my cheek. 'Come along,' she says. 'We haven't far to go.'

II.

We are staying in a modern, semi-detached cottage on a campsite next to the lake. An agreeable breeze rustles the trees overhead and the light is dazzling gold, interrupted by occasional lapis hues. The cottage has one decent-sized bedroom and one spacious kitchen-cum-living room, double height with a loft area for more guests. This opens out onto a quaint deck with view of the water's edge and a sunken brook but – and this is most important – like any self-respecting Finnish abode, it has a sauna and wet room. As I am not one to do without creature comforts, this choice of residence suits me fine. I am already picturing myself typing up my review with a cup of coffee at the small wrought-iron table on the terrace, my scolding critique tempered by the lake's gentle breath. My reverie is broken, however, as we have to get a move on. We have guests tonight. This was my wife's university town a decade ago, and she has many friends to catch up with.

I am, how should I put this delicately, not amused at our mode of transport for the weekend. I haven't ridden a bicycle since I was in school and, while you never forget the *how*, the *why* doesn't come back immediately. It doesn't help that my bike has no gears, a jammed seat that is about two inches too high and a reverse-pedal braking system. Yet I soon find myself careening through the grid that makes up Joensuu. The streets are a patchwork of conflicting architectural opinions, bordered by nature's majesty. Modern apartment blocks sit noisily next to older versions which, in turn, look down upon the traditional wooden mansions that, despite their varying degrees of neglect, bookend many of the streets, eyeing passers-by with their elegance and quiet authority. We ride the slight incline of Papinkatu, past the imposing gothic revival Lutheran church and turn left along Kauppakatu and into the Joensuun Tori.

This wide market is teeming every day of the summer with locals selling crafts, antiques and foods ranging from the traditional to the exotic. The market is flanked on the north and south by generic modern façades housing shops, offices and apartments and adorned with backlit signs advertising the stores therein. The western side houses a pedestrian thoroughfare that is home to a competitive version of street hockey this weekend and has a view of the Joensuun Taidemuseo or art museum. The eastern side is dominated by the Joensuun Kaupungintalo or theatre. In the centre of the market is a large teepee that is home to a temporary bar and cafe. We escape the heat here and order up a non-alcoholic beer for me and a sparkling water for the wife. After this pit stop, we take a brief turn around the market, eyeing and fingering the wares. My wife excitedly points out the traditional dishes, and we resolve to pick up a few of the local Karelian pies. These are rye-bread delicacies that are somewhat suggestive of ladies' nethers, filled with rice pudding and topped with dollops of egg butter.

We take our bikes again and peddle for the Suvantokatu and over the high bridge. Stopping at the midpoint, my wife points out that in the winter the temperatures can drop to -40° Celsius, and the wind on the bridge can kill. An arresting thought, and I try to juxtapose the experience of cycling in +30° Celsius with standing stock still in the other. We ride a little further but stop for an ice cream in the courtyard of an apartment block where she used to live. The silence again descends like an unwelcome fly buzzing about and landing uninvited. I watch my wife absentmindedly pick the chocolate from her ice cream as she obviously relives one or more memories from this exact spot on a swing chair beneath a birch canopy. Unexpectedly, I feel the first sprig of affection for Joensuu. We pedal on along the east bank of the river, taking in the ancient train station, with its parked and preserved steam locomotive, cross the railway bridge and circle back to an indoor flea market, where we pick up a heart-shaped wicker basket to hold the Belgian treats we will give to my wife's friends for their wedding tomorrow.

Back at the cottage we prepare for the arrival of the evening's guests. Tiia is a bubbly local beekeeper with pale blonde hair and light blue eyes. She laughs freely and wears a clement smile. She is first out of the clapped-out VW wagon (circa 1980), and her arms wrap solidly about my wife in a very genuine embrace. Paul is her English (somewhere in the north) boyfriend. He is sinewy and wears the buff hue of someone used to working outdoors, in this case, beekeeping and busking. I proffer an outstretched hand for a shake, but he counters with a familiar, masculine – if somewhat awkward – hug.

We sit and eat homemade guacamole and nachos and sip beers, ciders and sparkling wine. I made the guacamole despite my aversion to avocado, and I appear to be quite good at it. The added bonus being the opportunity to slice and peel a most hated culinary foe and smash it with as much force as I could muster. When an acceptable mush, I press another offensive food in with similar gusto: tomato. One of nature's great fence sitters, it plays both sides, not sweet and enticing like a fruit and without the ruthless nutrition of a vegetable. I expound on this to our guests, who laugh, and I even draw an unwilling smile from my wife. I am good around people. I can always draw a genuine chuckle from a stranger.

We decide to take a dip in the lake before the sauna, so we take turns changing into our trunks and bikinis while I fire up the sauna. I steal a glimpse at my wife in the bed-room, her long limbs stretching and arching, covered in her milky skin. Paul calls me back to the land of the living. He has brought his steel six-string to the terrace and is belting out a bluesy rendition of Van Morrison's 'Moondance'. A hedgehog ambles past unconcerned. We walk down to the beach and observe the youth playing volleyball on the hot sand. I reach for my wife's hand and our fingers brush, but she skips out toward the water's edge ahead of me. She delicately dips a toe in and squeals with mock terror and secret delight at the chill. Paul and I suck in lungfuls of air and, without a word, race like children into the depths. Rising up and pushing the hair back over my scalp I take in the silhouetted shoreline of spruce set against the cerulean lake as the golden sphere slowly falling from above. Children squeal as fathers tumble as monstrous krakens rising after them from the depths. Something within me stirs. Just a bud of a notion of an idea dreamt by a younger and more daring me. Perhaps, perhaps I would like to have this. This family, this lake, this life. I shake it off.

The sauna is pushing 70° Celsius when we've showered and taken our places. A bucket of birch branches soaking in water rests on the lower step, and we take turns flagellating ourselves. It's supposedly good for circulation. I can't speak to that, but I can confirm that it reddens and irritates the skin.

After the sauna, we suit up to head back into town. Paul is going busking on a stretch of the market, and we decide to tag along for support and to sample a little of the Joensuu nightlife.

The wife and I take our steel two-wheeled chariots and park outside the fast-food restaurant she called work so many years ago. The Dolly Burger. We find Paul perched in front of the Pizza Buffet, already belting out a Robert Johnson classic when a relatively impaired young woman approaches him. 'Can I be your dancer?' she shrieks and, without encouragement or rhythm, begins to gyrate in a fashion unsuited to the Delta blues. Her movements, though not graceful, do have the effect of arresting the male traffic passing by and, before long, the gentle chime of coin on coin ceases as notes are placed in Paul's upturned cap. One man drops a two-euro coin shy of the target and our fearless dancer bends double to retrieve it, giving Tiia, my wife and I a full view, nothing left to the imagination. The girl then resumes the vertical, oblivious, and to shocked laughter. We decide to call it a night.

III.

The morning finds me naked and riddled with mosquito punctures, which I do not mind so much as long as they have the grace to be silent as they dine. There is plenty of me to go around and I am content in my largesse so long as my sleep is not interrupted. My wife is still slumbering and I bend and kiss her forehead as I steal in to the kitchen to make coffee. While waiting, I look myself over in the bathroom. Since I've stopped drinking, I have unburdened myself of ten kilos, and my eyes are generally white and not pink with red inkblots. My breathing is easier today, and my hair is less lank and pathetic. I am relaxing? What has the loch done to me? Reasonably pleased with my progress, I march in quiet triumph to the terrace and, coffee beaker and cup in hand, set myself up for some work time.

'. . . in addition to being a morally deficient specimen, Jack Kennedy was a physical and, no doubt intellectual, also-ran . . .'

When my beloved arises, I quickly pour her a cup of coffee and wash some raspberries to go in her yoghurt. In the microwave, I heat a stale, sugar-coated Belgian waffle that I had in my backpack, and we eat in near silence. Then she microwaves two Karelian pies, which are disposed of quickly. On a wedding day, you never really know how long it will be before your next meal. We shower, we dress. I am suited and booted in a white shirt with blue check, a mustard-yellow knitted tie and dark fuchsia slacks. My wife is pure elegance in Perse silk, shoulders exposed; heads will turn throughout the day when she walks by. We are forced to saddle up and head to the market so that my wife can have her hair coiffed and nailed up as befits her. In the meantime, I fetch some ribbon to add to the Belgian hamper. A beautiful basket of Belgian chocolates, Speculoos spreads, beers and schnapps. Afterwards, I sit and have a coffee out of the glare of the sun, under the protective wings of the teepee. I collect her from the hairdresser, and we glide along toward the church.

My wife spots some old classmates hiding under the shade of a tree, and she hurries over with me in full puppy-dog mode behind. I nod and smile as I am trained to do. Not speaking the language limits conversation and, although Finns generally speak English, they are not the most gregarious of people. Looking about, I study the faces, trying to separate family from friend. It's purely a guessing game, as I don't know a soul here and am fully prepared to fend for myself throughout the day. We move inside after the pleasantries and brief biographical updates and find a nice cool pew.

The church is relatively Spartan but has distinct New England decorative features or, at least, what Hollywood has taught me to be of New England. Behind the altar is a large fresco of the Crucifixion, and the ceiling is an impressive painted canopy of interwoven ivy. The groom rises on the command of the organ: tall, bear-like, blonde and gallant-looking in traditional Victorian wedding attire. The bride is led up the aisle, blushing in white silk and embroidery, with a shock of crimson hair tumbling to one side and down her shoulder. The ceremony is short, simple and blessedly all about the couple. After vows are sworn, rings are exchanged and then it is a simple kiss and the newlywed couple proceed outside with the guests falling in behind, blowing bubbles from little canisters while the photographer tries to grab every shot she can. We hitch a ride to the reception with two of my wife's old class friends: Reija and Jarno, a short-of-stature couple with the distinction of not being in any way distinct.

The dinner and reception are held on a rustic old farm on the far side of the lake. A renovated barn houses the brunt of festivities. Two long white-clad tables, adorned in pink, are lined up in the annex. The walking dinner is comprised of traditional steaming vegetable stews, succulent meat dishes, creamy sauces, fresh salads and Karelian pies. Deserts follow in rich succession, and all is helped along with free-flowing wine, the notorious Finnish gin concoction known as 'long drink' and, for me, a sweet, non-alcoholic ale that is extremely easy to imbibe. There are no speeches, just laughter from the groom. The party eventually dissolves and small cliques begin forming.

The groom suddenly asks if any of the male coterie can help him with 'paperwork', and a conspiring look falls over the men present. The women roll their eyes in mock exasperation before shooing their dates out. Just as I am about to take my seat, another member of the party approaches and asks me to join. My wife smiles and, with a shooing motion I too am banished to do the 'paperwork'. A wave of apprehension sweeps over me as I try to imagine the incredulous faces of the hard-drinking Finns as I explain that the only foreigner, an Irishman, does not partake. We tumble along down a grass verge, away from the clamour of the other celebrants and come to a stop in front of a high, windowless barn, even more ancient than the other farm structures. A small door is opened and my guide ducks inside. I follow and am greeted by the sight of nearly all of the male guests bent low over dark wooden tables, pouring glasses of Scotch and vodka and Kossu into crystal tumblers. One member of this exclusive club is handing out cigars, and this picture is watched from above by a framed scene from an imaginary card game between Marilyn Monroe, Humphrey Bogart, James Dean and Elvis. A cigar and a tumbler are pushed my way but, with careful dexterity, I accept the finest of Havana while rejecting Scotland's charm. This is spotted by the groom who simply shrugs and continues extolling the merits of whiskey over vodka, or I assume as much – the conversation is taking place in Finnish, after all.

We then step outside, away from the natural tar perfume of the cabin, to enjoy the chosen poisons in the now cooling air. I take a pull from the cigar and the cloud is rich, warm and fragrant with vanilla. Laughter erupts as one of the more inebriated gents falls backward on his arse but, with practiced skill, spills not a drop. The conversation begins to open up and, before I know it, the alien tongue has transferred into something familiar, as I am being jabbed and jibed in my own native speech. The reticent Finnish male needs only a drop or two of Dutch courage before he blooms.

Before long, we are being summoned by the expectant females. The traditional bouquet-throwing is about to begin. We wade around the excited school of unwed women and take our places. Who among my newfound northern brothers will be next down the aisle depends, as tradition goes, on the flight of a bouquet of flowers and the speed and strength of his chosen cohort. The bride mounts the ramp toward the upper level of the barn. She looks back with a sly grin and winks at the assembled. Her arms clasp the stem of the bouquet and with flurry of speed and silk, the bouquet is sent skyward in a ferocious arc. The women push and pull, but the bouquet has chosen and, with a little backspin, seems to evade several hands before landing in the clutches of Reija. I turn to Jarno, his head drops.

I find my wife's gaze, her green eyes alive with delight. I laugh. It's a laugh I have not heard in a long time. Free and clear and innocent.

Moments later, I am told to take the place of the women, as another tradition must unfold. The throwing of the bride's garter. The groom bends low on the ramp and burrows beneath the rows of embroidered cloth while the bride again offers up a knowing and suggestive wink. He stoops before emerging, triumphant, with the circular ribbon in his hand. With little ceremony, he turns his back on his congregation and tosses the garter skyward. This arc is more at the mercy of the breeze and falls short to the front row. A grunt and grab are all it takes for the winner to step forward. A round of applause and a bow and this part of the festivities has come to an end.

The band strikes up and we tread up the stone ramp to the upper level of the barn, the steep climb forcing gallantry upon the men as ladies grab for steady arms, this being no place for heels. Inside, the band breaks into a decade-old chart hit, and the heavily worn dance floor begins to fill. A bow-tied barman stands behind a rustic counter and begins mixing some prearranged menu. Before the night is through, these will be mutated and experimented with until the taste-to-toxicity ratio favours the latter.

I find my wife as the bride and groom have their first dance and we take our cue when the bridal party have joined. I hold her tight and kiss her often. The music ranges from soft to animated to bizarre, as the orange-and-red evening gives way to the lavender-and-lilac night. The sky breaks out in stars as we say our goodbyes with hugs, handshakes and next-time-in-Brusselses. We head back with Reija and Jarno, reliving the funnier incidents. In the distance, a single column of white clouds floats on the lake. Silently, the giant trundles in our direction until a flash of crimson ignites its recesses and a ribbon of flaming doom shoots downward. We miss the clap of Thor that follows, but are mesmerised by the sight.

Back in the market, we opt to grab a Dolly Burger purely for the novelty. Then we cycle home through the darkened streets in full formal attire, a little less polished, but feeling so much younger.

At the cabin, we unfold the spoils of the burger bar. My wife has a slim vegetarian sandwich, sensible and delicious. I opted for the Äijä (Dude) Burger. I unfold the wrapping to reveal a colossus of stinking meat and bread. Spicy lamb kebab and bacon and beef covered in processed cheese, with a slice of buffalo tomato and a leaf of lettuce. I finish it but will surely pay and pay dearly tomorrow.

We check our bags once more, to make sure nothing will be left behind. I double-check again and yet I am ill at ease. I have neglected my review. More importantly, I have neglected the Internet and my connection with civilisation. I have not rushed quickly through a city street or huddled inside a metro car either. And I have not missed it.

Teeth brushed, we climb into bed. The heat is swept around by the table-top fan, and my wife leans her head close as she drifts away in peaceful slumber, exhausted from dancing and drink, food and laughter. The morning will be upon us early, and the blitz of travel, but even so I cannot sleep. It's not that my stomach is hard at work. I have taken on extra heavy fuel, but something is standing sentinel at the gates of Somnus's lair. It will not let me pass. I climb from the bed and walk to the kitchen to fetch a glass of water, but I am instead drawn toward the terrace. I step outside and allow the cool night air to sweep across me. For some inexplicable reason, I am drawn forward and step down onto the grass.

The blades bow underfoot or sneak finely between my toes. I inhale slowly, deeply. The night, this Finnish night, is intoxicating. More so than any beer or wine or spirit. I suddenly notice that I am not alone. A hare has stopped close by and is eyeing me with suspicion. I refrain from any inane attempts to call it closer and we simply watch each another. Suddenly, his ears prick and he scurries away. Then, nothing. Silence and darkness and a stillness unlike any I have known before. It begins to overwhelm me. A dull thud at first. For a moment I think that some pock-faced teen in a Toyota Starlet with speakers that cost more than the car is drawing near, but no. It's something else, something loud. A vacuous siren calling. A call not unlike the terror you experience when standing at the shore looking out into an ocean. A seething emptiness in which you are nothing.

I begin to sweat, heat rising within. My breathing becomes erratic and I drop to my knees. I begin to cough and choke and panic. On all fours, I feel a fever rest its hands on me and, in my terror, I look for calm and coolness. I crawl toward the small brook by the cabin. I have become one of the night creatures, fur and freedom. This is my territory. When men sleep I reign. I edge closer until the silver lie of the moon's light shows a distorted reflection of my face. I dry heave, I cough and I plunge my steaming head into the cool stream. Silence . . . and then I die. 'The calm/Cool face of the water/Asked me for a kiss.'

In the darkness all is mute, my senses frozen as the water quells the inferno burning within. With a sweep, I emerge again, gasping. Straining for air and life. Ready to scream and cry. I feel alive, more alive than I have in years. I slump back onto the grass and, dripping wet, I begin to laugh. A quiet laugh. A confident, self-assured laugh. The laugh of contentment. I wonder if this is what birth feels like. If you have a few moments of infantile clarity when you emerge from your mother's womb. Is this the sensation you feel? All ice and fire and fitful breaths. Breathing for the first time. I stand as if I were a toddler pulling myself up as I had seen my parents do so many times before. Is this what that feels like? I take a tentative and unsteady step, then another, then another. I almost lose control but manage to reach for the balustrade of the terrace and steady myself. I survey the black void of the lake, its midnight-and-amethyst solidity broken only by the treacherous moon. I am alive. I died and now I am alive. I have been reborn, at the mouth of the river.

8.
The Manila Envelope
Tendayi Bloom

I hadn't really believed Mom would come, but, standing in line in the wings of the Holy Family Ceremonial Hall – the big wooden room by the library – it's hard not to hope. Stepping out onto the platform when my name's called, I can't stop myself scanning the faces, willing Mom's to be among them, then sagging when it's clear she's not there. Shaking Ms Navarro's hand, it takes all my energy to hold back the tears. I take the book and certificate without looking at them. Once back among the rows of girls below the stage, I shove them under my seat and slump back, biting my lip, kneading my fingers.

What was it Mom said after that first awards ceremony?

'That certificate is by rights your dad's.'

And, later: 'Smiling at your success? You glad he's gone?'

Like every year, I wish I could swap the awards, the good school, the bedroom of my own, everything, for Dad to put his hand on my head like before, and for him to make Mom smile.

Like every year, as the ceremony closes, Ms Navarro invites the girls to join their families for snacks in the staff area of the canteen. It's a big honour, but I don't stay to see my friends gush together with their moms and dads and younger siblings. Most of them have parents working overseas, but they also have moms, dads, aunties and uncles who come to awards ceremonies.

I shove my prize into my school bag, wincing a little as the certificate crumples, and walk straight out of the gates. The other students, those who haven't won anything, are already on the way back to lessons, so there's no one but the guards in their uniforms, shiny badges and crisp hats, to see me leave. They know me by name, know I'm not a troublemaker, and let me go, no questions. Robby raises his hand in a wave, but I can't face talking to either of them today.

As it's early to be leaving, there's only one tricycle waiting outside the gates, and I swing into the small green carriage alone, enjoying having the cushion and sunshade to myself. The boy pedalling isn't much older than me. His faded t-shirt is speckled with small holes from sweat and over-washing. It contrasts with the modest front trim of my crisp white blouse, with its small white buttons and gathered sleeves. The boy's skin is dark and pockmarked, and his calf muscles tense and loosen like machines as his feet work the pedals along one of Metromanila's big residential highways to our building. Down the back of his right leg, amidst the dust, the pink scarring of old insect bites, and the scattered adolescent hair, is the word 'J E S U S', in the uneven black of a street tattoo.

From where I sit, to his right, below and behind, I can just make out his profile: his lashes and his soft stubble. The set of his mouth is thoughtful, but his eyes seem unfocussed. His mind must be elsewhere. I wonder where he lives.

Rather than be dropped off directly at home, I tell him to

stop at the noodle bar. I give him a handful of pesos and go in. Ordering up *pancit molo*, I sit on one of the tall stools at the bar, where I can watch the American actors and actresses on the TV screen, their moving mouths at odds with the love ballads droning overhead. The pleats of my blue college skirt stretch across my thighs, and I surprise myself by undoing the top buttons of my blouse, which feels tighter than usual around my throat. I trace the fake wood pattern in the countertop with my finger as I wait for my soup.

A man comes in and sits at the next stool. His skin and face are Filipino, but he holds himself like a foreigner: easy, filling his territory. His hair is just long enough to have that tousled look and his skin is smooth and shaven He has the smallest of lines at the corners of his eyes and in his forehead. It makes him look interesting, like he knows more than the teenage boys you meet, but he still isn't old. As he settles, a waft of foreign aftershave passes over the rich food smells of the shop. His blue suit jacket is made of that material that always seems ironed. The heavy-looking buttons are golden. He wears a pale blue shirt, with the collar undone. He asks the owner for pork-dumpling soup and turns to me, leaning over.

'You can't beat homemade *pancit molo*.'

It feels like I'm in a film. On a normal day, I'd probably be embarrassed if a strange man sat down next to me and started to talk. But my mind's still fuzzy from what happened at the ceremony, and I feel like playing along. When he asks where I work, his voice has that smooth, regular American sound to it. My cheeks get warm because he thinks I'm mature enough to be working. They burn a little deeper as I follow his eyes to the college crest on my blouse, glad I opened the buttons. I lie that I'm in the final year. When my soup comes, I don't know whether to wait for him before starting. I don't want to presume we're eating together, so I take up the spoon.

The soup's salty and sharp, helping a little against the intense heat of the shop. Leaning over the steaming bowl, I notice the sweat droplets forming between my breasts. The man moves his stool a little closer. It's only a centimetre or so but it feels significant.

'I'm Michael,' he says. 'You?'

I don't know how to respond. The shop owner arrives and slides the man's soup across the counter to him. Michael reaches forward, taking a thick, rough-cut noodle that's escaping down the side of the bowl with his fingers. Letting drips fall, he brings it towards himself, lowering it into his mouth. I can't say anything at all. I can't look away.

Finally, I say, 'Teresa Lee. My name, sir. It's Teresa Lee.'

And I watch his face.

He doesn't seem to disapprove and it feels good to think I've pleased him.

Soup finished, I'm still pulling my spoon over the dregs, cupping the bowl. Michael turns to face me and slides his hand over, touching the back of my wrist. His hand is surprisingly small and childlike. The fingers are short, the nails stubby. I find myself staring at it.

He looks embarrassed.

'Pardon me, ma'am, but could we meet again?'

Without waiting for an answer, he puts a business card on the counter between us, with his other hand. A real business card. Then he pays for both soups and smiles right into my eyes.

'Call me,' he says.

And leaves.

The next day is Friday, and I can't stop thinking about him, his dark eyes, the way his brows curve, the feel of his small fingers touching mine. It takes all the way to the early evening to gather the courage to call him. I lay the card on the table in the hallway.

MICHAEL FERNANDEZ
BUSINESS EXECUTIVE

There's a Manila cell phone number. I lift the receiver. Mom's lying on the couch in the next room. José is down the hall. I almost hang up when Michael answers. But I stop myself. He sounds happy to hear from me and, feeling my face getting red again, I'm glad we're separated by telephone wires.

He tells me to meet him the next day, at the entrance to Rizal Park in the Intramuros part of the city, so we can get to know each other. I haven't been there since I went with Dad as a little kid. I haven't ventured as far as the Old City since then. I try not to sound nervous as he explains about the LRT stop, and I work hard to remember the directions.

The next day, I panic about what to wear, finally settling on jeans and a T-shirt. I set out early to avoid the crush of people. It's only when I arrive that it hits me that my brother's never been here, where his namesake, José Rizal, breathed his last breaths and became a national hero. Part of me feels guilty, wishing I'd brought him along. But at the same time, I'm glad I didn't.

For José, it's different. He doesn't remember when Mom

used to smile. All he knows is the mausoleum with closed windows and air conditioning, which feels dark and dead. For José, that life's normal. He probably wouldn't even recognise Dad if he walked right in the door. To be honest, I've always been kind of jealous of him for that. I'm thinking about all this when Michael comes around the very corner he'd said he would. And I'm back in the same film as before.

He smiles with eyes that have seen the world. Taking my hand, he leads me around the park, pointing things out. He knows so much, has read so much. It's amazing. As we're walking, I talk more about my family, about Dad.

'How'd you like to come to New York yourself?'

My breath catches. I daren't believe I'm hearing right. This really is like being in a film.

'I know a family out there, right in Central Park, near the Statue of Liberty, that needs someone to mind their two little boys, help them with their homework, do a bit of dusting. Look, sorry if it's out of place, but if that's something that might interest you, they need someone quickly. I can put in a word.'

We're walking on the tarmac area between the buildings of the park, where you could imagine the rallies and speeches from history class. It's there, by the national monument, with the flowers blooming and all the people strolling back and forth, that he turns to me. He looks younger. Nervous. He strokes my chin gently, lifting it, and before I know what's happening, he kisses me gently on the lips. I feel dizzy.

Then, with his face still close, he adds: 'If I'm honest, it's selfishness. I'd love you to come to New York. There's so much I could show you there.'

I feel so many things it is hard to understand. It's less than forty-eight hours since we met, but my world has swung in a way I could never have imagined, and it can't swing back. My mind is full of pictures of Dad so happy to see me and of me telling José all the things that I've done and seen. I imagine holding hands with Michael, walking through the pictures on the postcards Dad stopped sending years ago.

Exploding through everything, though, making everything else faded or black-and-white is the feeling in my chest of his lips on mine. Nothing's quite real. Nothing has consequences. I know that this is what love must feel like.

The next day is Sunday and Father Patrice is talking to his flock over the shuffling of hand fans and the crying of a baby in the back. I'm not quite sure why I came. Mom gradually stopped bringing José to church ages ago, and it's probably been two Christmases since we've been, the three of us, as a family.

'We mustn't wait for the Lord to speak with words,' Father Patrice declares. 'He may send us a messenger or give us a sign. We mustn't be afraid. God is all-encompassing. Brothers and sisters we must believe in that love. We must follow it.'

As Father Patrice is talking, all I can think of are the Bible stories of people who leave their homes to follow messengers. The congregation stands for the hymn. It is 'Love Divine'. And I stand with them. I open and close my mouth like a fish. Perhaps I sing, but I don't notice. I know now I'm making the right decision.

★

The driver revs, frustrated at the Monday-afternoon Manila traffic. Behind, my right temple flattened against the window, I gaze absently through the dusk. Outside, the red smile of the Jollibee's Bee welcomes post-work burger-grabbers. I let my jaw hang, not knowing what to feel. Beside me, the man's aftershave smells no less exotic than when I first smelt it. We're no longer holding hands. He doesn't seem to notice.

The lights change. The taxi pulls away, wooden rosary clacking against the rear-view mirror, crucifix hanging askew like a misshapen kiss. Outside, Mother Mary stands twenty feet tall, wrapped in multi-coloured blinking lights. Her face is impassive, her hands outstretched. She's making sure that everything is okay. Behind her is some military building. On either side, ornamental plinths display ornamental mounted guns. I turn my eyes to my hands, palms down, resting on my school bag. I can't quite believe that less than half an hour ago I was at home. It feels like a thousand years.

Mom said nothing when I left. Nothing. When I told her where I was going she didn't even sit up from the mattress. Tears dribbled down her face. Useless. We didn't hug. I don't quite know what I expected, but it wrong-footed me. I figure Mom's probably still lying there while I sit slumped and small in the back of a white cab, her only daughter, telling myself I'm making the right decision. I *have* made the right decision.

José'll probably arrive home about now from some sports practice or other. What'll Mom tell him? Probably she'll say nothing at all, like when Dad left. I wish I'd known how to tell him myself.

In the car, Michael still isn't looking at me and I turn again to the window. The city outside already feels far away, as I catch glimpses of lives being lived in a poor stretch of town. By the roadside, a pregnant woman leans against a scraggly tree trunk, right hand protecting her swollen belly, left laying, palm out, across her face. Behind her, a father combs a small child's hair, while three others bounce on the bare branch of the sparse city tree: a family, together. Not much further on, a group of construction workers sit outside a noodle shop, white bowls in strong left hands, right hands gesticulating, scooping food and resting on tables. Above them, a sign flickers with pictures of dumplings. Today must be a celebration. They can't be on more than 200 pesos a day, and that place probably cost at least forty.

A dull pop brings me back to the taxi, and I catch the driver using his tongue to gather the pink aftermath of bubblegum from his lips, and then continuing to chew. I hadn't noticed his chewing before, but now it squelches loudly behind the grainy fizzle of American pop music. I study his face in the mirror, but he doesn't meet my eyes. Between the strings of brown beads, the muscles of his jaw work the gum in an endless, unproductive effort. Emerging behind him, the mirror shows the sleeve of Michael's suit jacket.

Outside, through the window, the multi-carriageway joins the highway and our battered white taxi rises above the city, onto the overpass. The blinking lights of a plane move steady overhead. Not far now. Outside, shacks, piled high, drip corrugated metal roofs, and bedraggled clothing hangs to dry. Points of light glow out of the gloom of the now-gathered dusk. I imagine Mom, a country girl, eighteen years old, leaving the open air of the paddy to join her husband in those grimy shacks that grow like plaque between the districts of the city. I think of Michael. But I don't turn from the window.

On a large billboard, a fat man, fifteen metres tall in his chef's hat, licks his lips, surrounded by blackened meat, under the orange-and-black inscription 'Gerry's Grill . . . meat for everyone!' Another up-lit poster, several stories high, proclaiming 'Manhattan Garden City', rises above the dirty grey of real life below.

Without ceremony, the shacks subside, replaced again by the apartment blocks of the families of overseas Filipino workers, 'OFWs'. This neighbourhood looks more like mine. McDonald's, Jollibees, Dairy Queen, and KFC fill the district with the red lights of progress and money from abroad. Behind the many windows, incomplete families are cooking and doing homework and waiting for letters, phone calls, emails and money from far away.

The taxi dives down from the overpass into a tunnel. Michael continues to sit beside me. I try to understand his silence. Without the city to focus on, my hair prickles. My ears are now filling with the whoosh of the tunnel. My mind still feels empty and full, like when you're a kid and you put too much rice in your mouth, so you can't swallow. The tunnel glows sparse yellow.

A decorated jeepney passes. In the back, visible through the open doors, a blue-ribboned girl sleeps, slung forward and prone across her father's lap. Although the van is full, the pair are in a separate world; the father's hand, protective, rests between the child's shoulder blades. The jeepney bounces in a pothole, but still she sleeps, in complete trust, across his knees.

I realise I wish me and Michael were still holding hands. It had been reassuring. But something stops me from reaching across.

Leaving the tunnel, the taxi manoeuvres off the main road. It putters to a halt in an isolated corner of a vast car park. Overhead, an airplane climbs, shrinking until it is just the blipping of its wing lights.

The driver steps from the car and leans back against the closed door, lighting a cigarette.

Michael takes a manila envelope from his inside pocket, unfolding it. He places it on the seat between us. It takes me a few seconds to realise it's a signal, and I hand him the roll of bills without looking at his face. It's the money I took from the bank account Dad set up, the 'university account'. I dug the paperwork from the desk drawers Saturday night after getting back from the Old City. Mom didn't even notice.

I'm embarrassed to hand it over at first. It's nowhere near enough to cover everything but, on Saturday, Michael had been so happy when I'd said I would come that he'd hugged me and reassured me that I could easily pay off the rest with my first pay cheques. He'd laughed when I'd said I felt bad taking the money meant for José.

'You'll fill the account ten times over with dollars, long before José finishes school.'

Now, I'm worried he'll have changed his mind. That he'll be cross.

But he isn't. He takes the money, counts it and puts it in his inside pocket. He doesn't say anything. I don't know what to do, so I turn my attention back down at my hands.

Michael touches my arm. I flinch. It's a gentle touch but

it doesn't feel how I expected. In the back seat, the intimacy is stifling. I shift my weight slightly and look between the scuffed plastic back of the seat in front me and my knitted fingers. It doesn't feel like it did in the Old City.

'When you arrive, you'll be met by Mr Tang. He's the one you'll be working for. I've got to finish some business here first.'

It's the first time he's spoken since we got in the car. His voice sounds foreign and smooth like before. Each word hangs in the air, weighted evenly. I'd assumed we'd be travelling together. I don't ask how I'll recognise Mr Tang. If I speak, I might break down. I don't acknowledge his words at all. Instead, I'm desperately thinking of the weekend, of his smile. The only thing that's the same is the feeling of being in a film.

Then Michael reaches right over me, so that his chest hovers over mine. I can feel his heat and smell his body underneath the perfume. He takes my right shoulder in his left hand, turning me slowly and firmly to face him. I can see stubble beginning to form on his neck. The skin there is looser than I remember.

'I'm only saying this 'cause I'm looking out for you,' he says.

In his voice is a conspiratorial smile. I raise my eyes slowly to take in his face again. The smile sits only on his lips. His eyes seem cold. I shiver. Had they always been like that and I just hadn't noticed? As soon as the thought occurs to me, though, I forget it.

He goes on.

'I've heard *such* stories about what happens to people who get found with false papers. You're lucky. Your visa's the best. No one will know unless you tell them. Stick with me and Mr Tang, and we'll look out for you. But find yourself talking to the police or anyone like that, and you're on your own, and wuh . . .'

He shakes his head solemnly, then adds:

'God help you!'

He crosses himself with his spare hand. The movement is awkward. His body is still spread across my side of the car. His weight falls briefly on my shoulder. For the second time in so few days, I am doing all I can to hold back the tears.

Inside the airport, winding queues are leading everywhere. There are uniforms and activity along the edges of the massive high-ceilinged hall, brightly lit and busy after the darkening night. The snakes of people shuffle slowly, swatting bugs and stirring clammy air with the large brown manila envelopes of OFWs. A group of foreign tourists stand awkwardly in one of the queues, unnaturally tall, with big luggage and thongs on their feet. Some people in darker uniforms patrol among the crowds. Sometimes they make marks on their clipboards. Sometimes they give instructions to the people around them.

Why did I bring my Holy Communion Bible instead of the Tagalog history book I won at the ceremony? The Bible's extra weight cuts into my shoulder. I fold my arms across my chest, around the manila envelope of documents. Truth is, I have to keep clutching it like that to stop my hands from shaking. I try to stand straight, to look like the woman Michael saw in me at the weekend. To try to feel like her too.

Michael's standing close behind me, and I reassure myself that this fast heart, this lack of breath, this pain in my chest, it's normal. It's just how love feels. To keep myself from running away, I concentrate on a pair of guys directly in front of me. They're older than me, but not much. They have sports bags at their feet, which they push along the ground as the line moves. One is done up with brown parcel tape. Either side of the tape, the broken zip sags. Their voices are quiet, like in a church, so I can't hear what they say except to know that they're from another island. They wear ironed shirts and baseball caps. The high ceiling makes them seem small, though they must both be taller than me by at least a head.

Focussing on the other travellers makes me feel calmer but, suddenly, Michael's hand is on my shoulder, directing me towards a desk that has become free. I tell myself his grip is reassuring. Behind the desk, a woman looks down. She is dressed like all the other women behind the desks to the right and to the left: red hat, white veil hanging from one side. The woman's smile is drawn on with perfect red lipstick that matches her hat. Her black eyeliner is immaculate.

'Your tickets, ma'am.'

I make to hand her the envelope. Once my hand has left my chest, it shakes freely and the envelope flaps at the woman, who snatches it, manicured nails tlacking against the paper.

The nothing inside now fills me in waves that threaten to make me black out, and I put my hand, empty of envelope, on the desk for support. Michael still stands behind, though now a few steps back. I can't tell if I miss his presence or feel relieved at the space. The woman with the perfect red lips takes an eternity to examine the contents and raises one of her perfect eyebrows when I confirm that my school bag is my only bag.

Stepping away from the desk, manila envelope again gripped to my chest, I almost fall into Michael, who takes my shoulder tightly and directs me around the winding queues. I nod and shake my head and reassure him that I don't have cold feet, and he kisses me gently on the forehead. It makes my heart beat even faster. I want to shout or hide, but don't know if it's from love or fear or something else entirely. I wish Mom had said something before I left.

Soon, we reach a pair of glass doors, sliding back and forth only slightly as each person passes through, never closing completely. He turns me to face him.

'We'll embrace goodbye here. When we next meet, we'll be in New York and we can start looking for your dad!'

He smiles again with his rubbery lips which have touched mine and pulls me to him. I turn my face aside and put my hands around his body in an embrace I've never given José, that I've dreamed of giving Dad. But I don't squeeze. I hold my breath against the exotic perfume under which I can now also identify nicotine and stale smells from the noodle shop. The rough lapel of his suit jacket pushes against my cheek and the unexpected bulge of his belt buckle feels uncomfortable against my stomach. It doesn't feel like they say in the magazines. To be honest, by now I just feel numb.

It's a long time before he loosens his arms enough to lean down and kiss me, this time wetly, on my closed lips. At the touch, something finally slices through me. I tell myself it isn't fear, that I'm too old to be so childish. This is love. It must be. He releases me. I walk like a drunk into the flow of people moving through the glass doors, and hear him saying he'll miss me, that we'll soon be eating pizza in New York, and that I'll introduce him to Dad. I don't turn.

Standing in the mass, the swaying light-headedness begins to subside, and I look around at the unsympathetic whiteness of the hall. The young men from before are a little ahead of me. Above them is a large plastic sign, swinging, with letters big and proud, 'OFW'. I wish I could just smile and be one of them, but something is holding me back. At the other end of the hall are more desks, and people fan out from the queue to stand at them, handing over their envelopes. Each desk has 'OFW' written across the top of the glass that separates the officials from the crowd. At the far corner, an identical desk invites, in multiple languages, 'all other passport holders', and a scanty line of foreigners wait by it, looking out of place.

I wish I could tell José about it. I'm surprised by how urgently I wish it. He'll be at home now. Wondering where I am. Maybe he's gone into my room to look for me. I wish I had left a note.

It is with this in my mind that I hand over the manila envelope for the second time. The official frowns and points to a small sign that asks passengers to take their documents out of their envelopes before coming to the counter. He clicks his tongue against the top of his mouth as he spreads the papers across his desk, shaking his head. I think of Michael crossing himself and the dizziness returns. I grab the side of the counter. The official looks up, but only for a second. As he focuses again on the papers, I try to interpret what had been in his eyes.

Finally, he gathers everything together, hands it back in

a pile with the envelope at the bottom, and tells me to go to gate T-3-4. Able again to breathe, I leave the desk, reciting 'T-3-4-T-3-4 . . .' to myself, looking desperately at the many signs suspended from the plasterboard ceiling, with arrows pointing here and there. I pass shops selling bags and bracelets and cigarettes and a big wooden mural map of the world. I stop only briefly to breathe the glorious, fresh saltiness of a noodle shop, and then continue again to follow signs, down some steps, under a blue billboard on which a happy woman in a northern city from a postcard declares, 'Non-bank remittance services you can trust'.

Relieved to be through the security checks, I start to feel anxious about Michael. I feel bad for mistrusting him even for a second, and I hope I still managed to say a proper goodbye. I hope he's not cross or upset, that he doesn't feel like I used him to get to go to New York. I resolve to buy him a present once I'm making money, in time to give to him when he comes. I wish he could be with me now, holding my hand.

Down the stairs, more kiosks sell snacks and I finally find myself at T-3-4. Someone lets me through a rope barrier into a seating area, where rows of plastic seats face a see-through plastic hoarding. In front of it stands an enormous flat-screen TV, flanked by glowing blue and white 'Samsung' hoardings. My jeans are sticking to the backs of my thighs.

At home, we've had cable TV for ages now, and I recognise the fast pace and commentator patter of an NBA game. Every few minutes, the game stops for American infomercials for slimming products or muscle enhancers. In some weird way, it reminds me of church, Father Patrice speaking about paradise or hope or something, with everyone facing the same way, feeling uncomfortable in the plastic seats. Like at chapel, I snatch glances at the people on either side of me. Some stare at their hands. Others talk urgently into mobile phones. They speak more openly than they usually would in public. In their voices, the same weight that hangs in the air over the pews.

My mind is filling with evenings without José, of conversations un-pursued with the girls at school, the teachers. There'll be no more awards ceremonies. And Mom will now lie alone, without a daughter to cook or talk to her. A chill is spreading through my belly and across my forehead. I try to remind myself about Mr Tang, and Dad, wherever he might be, and about Michael, who'll help me find him.

But, however much I try to be calm, what I'm doing suddenly seems enormous and I feel Dad, a decade ago, himself the child of an OFW, sitting in this seat, the same sweat sticking his jeans to his thighs, not knowing whether he would return. He hasn't.

The world feels heavy and inevitable. It's too late to change my mind.

People start passing by, on the other side of the hoarding in front of us. I try to see their faces through the thick plastic but I can't. Soon, the ladies in red hats with identical bright red lips start to float between the plastic seats, summoning groups of people by ticket numbers.

I stand stiffly when my number is called. There's nothing else I can do. I follow the others through the open gate to the hot tarmac, towards the metal steps. And so it is, uselessly looking around for a familiar face, that I take my last steps from the city.

9.
Kaveh Mirzaee and the Woman from Lashar
Lily Mabura

Kaveh Mirzaee was a miniature artist from Ābādān – that small island city between two rivers that flow into the Persian Gulf. The people of Ābādān love their city; it is a garden of palm trees edged with old wooden boats rocking in the surrounding waters. In Ābādān, one can smell the sea in the breeze and in the bounty of *hammour* and shrimp in the open fish markets. But Kaveh Mirzaee now lived away from Ābādān on the top floor of his building and kept to himself.

Being from Ābādān was not information he volunteered easily for he had seen the garden that was Ābādān torched and its oil refinery flaming red and black into the open skies of the gulf. Besides, the jokes that were made about people from Ābādān – with their Ray-Ban sunglasses, cowboy boots, obsession with soccer, *bandari* music, and a sweet tooth entirely devoted to doughnuts – was something he wished to avoid, even in jest. This, plus a host of other reasons, was behind his refusal to take part in an Eid progressive dinner with his neighbours.

Of course, it was absolutely true that, in his younger,

motor-biking years, he had been in possession of a second-hand pair of Ray-Ban sunglasses and a pair of black, lace-up Western boots that had matched his Kurdish riding pants. And that he had long harboured a dream of donning the yellow-and-blue uniform of Sanat Naft FC and celebrating match victories in a *bandari* den. Then the First Persian Gulf War had begun with the September Siege of Ābādān in 1980 and had dragged on for eight years. Nothing had remained the same after that war – it had ravaged the nation like leprosy ravages the body and leaves indelible marks.

This is how he had found himself living on a war-vet allowance in a government-subsidised studio miles away from Ābādān. His home was on a tree-lined street that meandered its way up to the Tochal look-out point in Tehran. The street had narrow *qanats* on either side, in which water ran down from the surrounding mountains, irrigating sycamore trees that towered as high as the buildings before branching out in a green profusion that arched over the street below. Traffic peaked in the early morning and evening hours, but it was ten o'clock now, and the traffic had eased out considerably, leaving the street to a group of construction workers, who were completing an old apartment block close by.

Such grand incompleteness this was: gray stone and concrete under scaffolding that had been weathered by Tehran's alternating harsh winters and summers into something of an old frock. 'Everything in the world,' the building seemed to say to Kaveh Mirzaee, 'is as incomplete as I am in this old frock that beats in the wind like a Qashqaee nomad's tent in the mountains. I wait out the winters like the nomads with their horses and cattle and sheep do in the valleys and then

hide away from the summer's high sun up in the mountains, seeking whatever grasses remain on the mountain
slopes and harvested wheat fields. Look around you and
you will see other incomplete buildings in this lull, Kaveh
Mirzaee – even incomplete people, for that matter, with
incomplete lives and incomplete hearts and incomplete
memories. Should not the construction workers be set on
this inherent incompleteness?'

The construction workers were mainly young Afghan
men who laboured in Tehran at the onset of spring and
wintered back home – ever on the road from one place to
another. Kaveh Mirzaee was seated at his desk, painting, the
adjacent window open to let in some fresh air, and could
hear these seasonal Afghans steeped in their work.

During the Siege of Ābādān, he had been taken prisoner
and held till the end of the war in a *shabestan* in Ramadi,
Iraq. The silence of the underground colonnaded brick
shabestan, which was all arches and domes, was only broken
by the howls of frequent gusts of wind that buffeted the
tower above and the slow, shuffling steps of the old man who
brought him food each day. It was for this reason that Kaveh
Mirzaee was a man attuned to sounds and smells. The noise
that the Afghans were making in the street below did not
disturb him at all. He listened to them hammer and drill and
lift and drop and call out to each other in all their youthful
zest, while that old frock of a scaffolding beat in the wind
and baked in the sun. In the midst of it all, he also heard
pigeons cooing in the sycamore trees close to his window.

Sometimes he left little pieces of bread on the windowsill
and he would watch the birds wheel down and peck at
them. When skies were red over Tehran, blighted by fierce

sandstorms blowing in from the deserts of Iraq, the pigeons not only pecked at the bread, but sometimes ventured in as well. They did so because they did not fear Kaveh Mirzaee – he had the stillness of the brick *shabestan* he had lived in for eight years within him; this stillness ran through his soul like the crescent dune fields of Rig-e Jenn in the Great Salt Desert, where not even the ancient caravan roads had ever crossed and nothing but wild spirits and onagers lived.

It was there in the way he moved. While neighbours hurriedly barred their windows and doors as the sandstorms blew in, Kaveh Mirzaee did so slowly, letting the pigeons in until the last minute. Then he would sit back with the pigeons about him and listen to the sand-laden storm toppling potted plants and garden statues from the balconies of his neighbourhood. There was nothing one could really do when it came to the storms and even less when it came to the fine sand they carried. It always found its way through all the barred doors and windows, seeping in through the finest of cracks. Later, one would find specks of sand on silk prayer rugs, under the fridge, in a barley sack, amongst rice cookies stored in a closed tin box in the larder, and in the pockets of winter coats stashed in the farthest corners of wardrobes. Kaveh Mirzaee moved quietly, hardly fretting, in the midst and aftermath of all this. Yes, so it was there in the way he moved and in the way he spoke – on the rare occasions that he did speak.

Because Kaveh Mirzaee had not yet stepped out to buy some bread this morning, there were no pigeons hovering at his window to be fed. He had hit his stride in his work and did not want to interrupt it with a walk to the bakery. He, instead, brewed some imported black Kenyan tea, which he usually purchased in small packets from the building's corner shop, and sweetened it with brown crystallised sugar.

He had been working for three straight hours when hunger set in. So he decided to take a shower and then head out to the bakery. Taking a shower was a ritual for Kaveh Mirzaee. When he had been unchained from the *shabestan* to be handed over to the Red Crescent for repatriation, his keepers, an elderly Iraqi Kurdish couple whose Ramadi country home and services had been requisitioned by the Iraqi army, had prepared a bath for him in a thick olive tree grove. He had cleansed himself under broken sunlight with rose-scented water and goat-milk soap, in a shelter of Ba'shiqa olive trees.

The elderly Kurdish couple had two sons: one had emigrated to Palestine, while the other had fallen in battle fighting for Iraqi troops. Kaveh Mirzaee had dressed with an assortment of these sons' clothes and left, a free man, in the Red Crescent van. From Ramadi, he had carried with him the stillness of the *shabestan* and everything that the old Kurdish man had taught him about miniature art. In memory of this day of freedom, Kaveh Mirzaee had decorated his Tehran bathroom with an olive-tree tile mosaic and used nothing but goat-milk soap for his skin, which had grown too sensitive for anything else.

These were the recurring memories occupying his mind when he stepped out of the bathroom, his trim black hair – shot through with silver – still wet, his pale skin moist, and the scent of goat-milk soap in the now humidified air. His bare feet had just touched the yellow Azarshahr travertine tile floor outside the bathroom when he noticed a sudden movement, only to realise that he had narrowly missed stepping on what looked like a snake.

He quickly stepped back into the bathroom, his equilibrium rattled. From behind the bathroom's glass door, he now saw that it was, indeed, a snake – a black snake with white marks around its nape. For a moment, he wondered how the snake had gotten into his studio. Then he realised the window facing his work desk was wide open. The snake must have gotten in through there by perhaps crossing from the overhanging sycamore tree branches to the open window's metallic frame. He could still hear the young Afghan men working and the pigeons cooing, but they would not be of help.

Eventually, the snake moved, sliding and slithering across the travertine tiles, towards his work desk, under his antique wooden chair, and, finally, onto the small, Kork wool rug underneath which it coiled. It took a long while to do this, and Kaveh Mirzaee patiently watched it as his hair and his skin dried out and the humidity in the studio dissipated and the young Afghans and the pigeons outside carried on as before.

When he felt safe enough, he opened the bathroom's glass door and hurried across the studio to his bed, where he had laid out his clothes. He got dressed much faster than usual, his eyes never leaving the snake. It seemed content, even peaceful, on that oval rug from Qom, which was patterned with white lotus flowers and green silk highlights. Kaveh Mirzaee put his sandals on – again, much faster than usual – and left his apartment without turning the key in the door. He had no clear plan for how to deal with the snake.

At a corner, on the way to the elevator, he bumped full speed into a woman. She was holding a brown grocery bag against her black *manteau*. The force of the impact made her drop the bag; spilling out, as if from a magician's hat, came a cascade of ripe tomatoes, eggplants, onions, potatoes and green herbs, and a huge packet of shredded Mozzarella cheese – menu ingredients, no doubt, for the Eid progressive dinner. The tomatoes, as ruby as Jupiter, radiated out across the floor like billiard balls, and Kaveh Mirzaee, momentarily embarrassed and clumsy, stepped on one and then the next.

'Madame,' he cried, 'I'm so sorry!' He squashed another tomato under his leather sandals, kicked at an eggplant like he was a marionette out of control, and was nearly undone by the hardness of a potato momentarily under one foot. 'Madame . . .'

She adjusted the matching chiffon *hijab* on her head and then assessed the damage done to her groceries – several of her tomatoes splayed out like starfish on the white linoleum floor, and Kaveh Mirzaee trying his best to get the rest of her groceries back into the bag.

'Thank you,' she said, taking the bag from him. 'You shouldn't worry . . .'

He looked at her face then and saw that it was as brown as the seeds of a Persian walnut. Her forehead was round and her lips were full and she carried the scent of *oud* about her.

'I will pay for this,' he said, dropping his gaze onto the wet redness on the floor, while feeling about for his wallet and not finding it.

'You are a war hero,' she said. 'You have already paid.'

He looked up at her, startled.

'Everybody in the building knows this, Kaveh Mirzaee, even those of us who are merely passing through.'

'I should pay, nonetheless,' he said, making his way back to his apartment for his wallet.

At the door, he, however, remembered the snake, momentarily forgotten amongst the red tomatoes and the woman with a brown face the colour of Persian walnut seeds. She is beautiful, Kaveh Mirzaee thought to himself, one hand on the doorknob.

She was watching him.

He stood there and did not open the door.

'They took away your family and everything that was dear to you in Ābādān. And yet you live, like a true *pahlevan*,' she said. 'The wind is in you, Kaveh Mirzaee – you shouldn't pay.'

'Oh . . . the wind . . . it must be coming from my window. I left it open.'

'I am from Lashar,' she said, 'and we hear the winds of Lashar just like my ancestors heard the winds of Africa. The wind I hear is *inside* of you.'

Kaveh Mirzaee looked into her eyes. They were deep in colour like dates from Bam and soft like only dates from Bam are.

'There is a snake in my apartment,' he said, when he could find his voice.

'A snake,' she said, with a growing smile. 'What colour is it?'

'Black . . . and white.'

'Open the door and let me see,' she said.

Kaveh Mirzaee opened the door and pointed to his work desk. The snake was still there, coiled on the oval rug.

She came to the open door and followed his gaze.

'It is a rat snake,' she said. 'You see them in the mountains . . . sometimes they find their way into people's houses and gardens. They are not poisonous.'

'They are not?'

'No, they aren't,' she said, putting down the grocery bag. 'They are like me – just passing through.'

She walked into his apartment like she was part of it. The snake on the rug did not move, and the hungry pigeons hovering on the windowsill did not flutter away. She knelt on the travertine floor and picked up the snake by its head without any hesitation whatsoever. It coiled around her arm like it was coiling around an old familiar tree branch, and stayed there – peaceful.

'See,' she said. 'It means no harm.'

There was nothing he could say.

She looked around his home and then at the samples of complete work on his desk: an old Sufi mystic, an antique silver teapot, a red lotus flower, the tragedy of Rostam and Sohrab, and a rendering of Vis and Rāmin in their love epic. Then she looked at the piles of camel-bone tiles with nothing on them, a drying palette of mixed water paints, liquid mother-of-pearl glowing in bottle and his array of tiny brushes made from the finest cat hair. She even turned the pages of his sketchbook, given to him by the old Kurdish man in Ramadi.

'Take something . . . anything,' he said to this woman from Lashar.

'Make me something new, Kaveh Mirzaee, and I will take it,' she said.

'Yes,' he said. And then he thought, *Yes, of course.*

She was like a desert wind that had not been barred outside, whose fine sands he would now forever find in the
depths of his being. His eyes followed her through the open
door. She left with the snake and her grocery bag and headed to the apartment at the end of the hallway.

Kaveh Mirzaee cleaned up the mess of crushed tomatoes
with a roll of tissue and then stood at his still wide-open
door thinking that he should go buy some bread now that
the snake had been taken care of. He picked up his wallet
from the night stand and turned the key in the lock. Walking
towards the elevator again, he found himself thinking about
the possibility of attending the Eid progressive dinner, as the
woman from Lashar was going to be there.

10.
In the Heat
Jackie Davis Martin

Her heels were getting crusty from the Athens dust. Walking the steep rubble of the Acropolis, the sun baking the tops of their heads, Charlotte thought about her feet again and reflexively flipped her leg at the knee and looked back: yes, her foot was uglier than it had been when she'd observed it late yesterday, her feet in the air above Neil, who had been grunting over her. He'd hate that what she was thinking of was her feet.

'A stone?' he asked. He reached to steady her.

Her skin was bare and hot and wet with sweat. They surveyed the jagged hill they'd traversed, the squares of white below, the hundreds of people like themselves swarming over the hillside. Neil pivoted them to see the Parthenon above.

'Not that far,' he said. He shook his shirt tails to let in a little air.

She squinted at the sun gleaming and flashing through the distant pillars and told him how thrilled she was with the sight. She knew he wanted her to be thrilled. And, mostly, she was. But she felt she was losing the capacity to thrill him.

It was not good to feel tested thousands of miles from home.

Three days before – when they first arrived in Athens – they'd been greeted by a tour guide, a lively woman with thick dark hair and thick round breasts that undulated as she gestured at the front of the bus. When she paused for breath she grasped the seats on either side of her, leaning forward, and invited the entire bus's inspection of the canyon of her cleavage. Even Charlotte was mesmerised by such a display, and Neil had mentioned it twice already.

She couldn't compete in any way with the tour guide's lusty glamour: she, Charlotte, the English teacher, the one who wanted to go to Greece because of *Oedipus* and *The Oresteia*.

The guide's name was Athena – Charlotte laughed when she heard it – and she'd bid farewell to their group to board another bus. Her aura, however, remained. Today, along with spaghetti sandals that invited crusty heels, Charlotte was wearing a strapless stretch jersey so her own bosom was loosened. Her shoulders were becoming burned.

After three years of dating, Neil admitted he had not been faithful. His confession to her of a dalliance had been tearful and dramatic and he'd begged her forgiveness. He said he loved only her, and Charlotte said she forgave him. The scene, occurring just six months ago, had been perhaps too dramatic, alarming her with a fear that she could lose Neil and also causing her to wonder why he was telling her such a thing. And why then. Had it happened before? She couldn't shake the suspicion that he'd shown a false contrition and would easily stray again.

'Let's rest a bit.' Neil sank onto a rock and nudged her down beside him. 'You have to do this sort of thing when you're young,' he said. They were thirty-seven and forty-three.

Young-ish. 'This heat. How do old people manage? They'd never see the Parthenon.'

Charlotte looked about. 'Tour buses? But they can't possibly reach the top.'

'She was something, wasn't she?'

Oh how stupid of her to mention tours, how rude of him.

'Athena,' he said, as though she'd forgotten.

Charlotte tugged at her stretch top and stood up. 'Shall we continue?'

Neil reached out both hands, interlocking them the way they did when they took hikes and assisted each other up steep terrains, and she pulled him upright. He pressed against her and smiled. The Parthenon itself was a way to go, the slag hillside pitching relentlessly uphill in the heat as they trudged to Charlotte's revered destination – ironically, the temple of Athena. There among the ruins shade was scant. Neil was excited at the friezes of the horses and warriors. Charlotte admired the maidens holding up the weight of the porch with their heads.

'I think they're not the real ones, though,' she said.

The descent was easier, but they were weary as they approached something like an ice cream stand.

'My brains feel fried,' Charlotte said. 'And it's all so foreign. What do you think that sign says?'

'Nitea,' Neil read. 'Maybe an orange drink. Like Fanta? Want one?'

He indicated to the vendor – the only way they communicated with the Greeks – two orange bottles in the cooler. In a tavern last night they'd pointed to a meat dish on another table, unable to discern anything familiar on the menu, and never did recognise it. Lamb? Beef? Goat?

The Plaka was stifling with its cacophonous piped music, jostling of crowds, leathers and incense stalls, and they were eager to return to their hotel room. But later, after showers, after lovemaking and another shower, they went back into the streets. They'd try a new *taverna*, they decided, strengthened enough by their familiar bodies to explore the foreign once again – and ventured into an alley strung with coloured lights. At the far end of the terrace of wooden tables, a folk band was playing – flutes and dulcimers – and they ordered beer and salads and bread. Charlotte grinned at Neil, swivelling on the bench to applaud the musicians, and, when she turned back, Neil's arms were extended in welcome to a woman who stood in the abstract circle of his embrace.

'Honey, it's Athena! She remembered us from the tour bus. You know – the first day?' He moved over and patted the space next to him.

What else could she say but, 'Of course. Join us, please.' Neil was happily flustered and ordered a round of *ouzo*. Athena looked freshly laundered in a blouse that resembled the aprons in the Agora, almost transparent. She loved Americans, she said, and was so happy to practice English. Her skin crinkled into smile wrinkles at the corners of her round eyes. Athena was probably her age, Charlotte realised. She sucked in her own stomach and sat higher

'Maybe Athena could show us around other parts of Athens?' Neil suggested. He laughed at the coincidence of the names, a stupid and conspicuous observation, Charlotte thought. Show them around? She and Neil and Athena together for a day? She kicked him under the table, but he was watching Athena.

'We were going to rent a car,' Neil said, pantomiming a steering wheel, 'and go to Delphi. Charlotte wants to see the theatre there. We'd pay you of course.'

Athena clasped her hands together and said she loved visiting Delphi. 'I feel so – what you say – with spirit,' she said. Her earrings, dangles of silver disks, reflected the tavern lights like little sparklers.

All Charlotte could picture was Neil behind the wheel he had just been faking, Athena gushing from the passenger side, and her crushed into a small back seat. And that was the way it happened.

The next day Athena was at the hotel desk at 6 AM, as Neil instructed, leaving Charlotte only the hours in between to protest.

'Relax, Char,' Neil had said, cuddling her in bed. He spoke with the expansiveness and generosity of a man about to date two women. 'It'll be fun; it'll be different. You liked her, too.'

'I did?'

But Neil had already dozed off and was soon snoring. Charlotte tossed fitfully and at some point poured herself whiskey from the flask Neil travelled with and stared at the moon over the Acropolis. The tiny balcony she stood on seemed symbolic of her life: she was in a place she longed to be, but merely hovering there, angry and helpless. She couldn't even read the letters of the language. She took another sip and turned to look at Neil, a man she loved, had loved. How could she get him to value her more? The curtains lifted in the filmy night breeze – it was all so romantic! She wanted to punish Neil for his thoughtlessness in inviting another woman – no matter whether she was a tour guide or not – into Athens, her dream destination. She felt like *stranding* him here. And suppose she did? Just for a little while, just for long enough for him to see that, without her, Charlotte, other women didn't mean much. She mulled over how she could do this.

Athena had shown up in a yellow sundress, her abundant hair piled on her head. Charlotte, in her T-shirt and shorts, felt relegated to the back seat on the basis of costume alone, the foster child of an exuberant couple. And, of course, Neil offered Athena the front seat – 'She needs to see where we're going, and Charlotte doesn't mind, do you, hon?'

'How much are you paying her?' Charlotte had asked at the car rental as Athena sat in the waiting room, her tanned legs crossed, her canvas sandals laced seductively around her ankles. Even her toes gleamed.

'Why would you concern yourself with that?' Neil had said. 'I've paid for everything, haven't I?'

Yes, of course he had. She knew that. Beholden was not a good position to be in. But what was? He'd reached for her in the dawn light and half asleep (finally), she'd succumbed to the familiar lovemaking, wondering only later whether he'd been fantasising about the buxom Athena.

Now, as the car rode precariously along the narrow mountain road so sparse of traffic that goats wandered by, Charlotte hugged her legs in the back seat, studying Neil's trim hair and Athena's coiled *mane*, and, as she took deep breaths of fear, reviewed what she could do. If necessary, if he continued to flirt, she could get the keys and drive back to the hotel. Or maybe just pretend to go on an errand – and what? – and disappear for a while.

Neil was addressing all his comments to Athena, as

though they were on a date. 'Do you have family here?' 'What sorts of things do you like to do when you're not tour guiding?' And, the one that made Charlotte laugh aloud, 'Do you go to Delphi often?' In all fairness, Athena sat at an angle in her front seat and talked over her shoulder to Charlotte as much as she could. A daughter. Grow plants – in pots. Dance. She'd been to Delphi four times before. It was beautiful. Top of the world. Charlotte, in her pique, fought against asking more, not wanting to give Neil the more rounded picture of this rounded female.

At a roadside stand (one could hardly even call it a cafe), where they stopped for a restroom (peeing in a hole in the ground) and Nescafé and cheese sandwiches at an outdoor table, Athena set them straight about the 'Nitea' sign.

'Pizza,' she said. 'Is saying 'pizza.' Here is frozen, put in oven, not made.'

Neil was delighted. 'That's great! Oh, I see. The "N" is really the "Pi" sign! Charlotte, look. Not an "E" but an "S", sigma. That's really funny.' He grasped Athena's knee through the sundress and shook it. 'Do you know what we thought?'

It was the first time he'd said 'we'. But he seemed to have forgotten who the 'we' was supposed to be. His hand lingered. Athena looked at his hand on her leg and then met his eyes. Charlotte felt a rush of anger. That anger – his causing her to consider a dramatic act – carried her through the hike to the top of the mountain. She carefully memorised the road they traversed, where they turned. But it was a monumental thing to do – to drive away!

On the top of Delphi the air and view filled her lungs and her head and, for a time, seemed to dissolve all else. The associations were magical: Parnassus, oracle, Apollo. She could be a believer in gods up here at Delphi. She gazed through the crumbling majestic pillars and altars to vast horizons of forests and mountain crags, to all of Greece, it seemed. Life seemed boundless in its opportunities for a moment, and the altitude dwarfed her petty jealousies. For a grand moment, she inhaled it all – blue sky, ruins – until she spotted Neil and Athena walking leisurely in the other direction, Athena pointing and Neil nodding and reaching around to steady her over uneven terrain. Charlotte started and gasped as she watched them growing smaller and smaller. She might have reached Delphi, but she stood here alone. Here, in the home of the gods, she was just a lowly mortal, a jealous one, one with keys in her pocket.

'Can I have the keys?' she'd asked Neil when they'd parked, hoping her voice hadn't quavered. 'In case I want to come get my extra shirt.'

She stumbled back down the grade they'd climbed as a threesome, skidding and slipping in the dust, her eyes blurred with tears of frustration and anger. She'd given Neil a little book about Delphi and he'd been enchanted – or so he'd said – saying that they'd experience its air – maybe he said 'spiritual air'– together. *Together.* She found the parking lot. The car was sitting on the tarmac, the sun's reflection against its metal blinding her even more. Could she drive it? The interior exhaled a thick heat.

Her breath came in gasps as she turned the key.

She exited the town of Delphi, a touristy place, entered the old road Athena had guided them to, and started the car winding down the mountain. She'd rehearsed the possibilities of today's bizarre actions in her head: she could drive the route back to Athens, park in the street, run up for her suitcase, get her passport, have the desk call a cab to the airport. On one level, it seemed like a plan; on another level, it seemed absolute folly.

She pictured Neil and Athena stranded on the mountaintop. Had he by now hidden behind one of Apollo's pillars to kiss her? Had he fondled her breasts? Who knew how many women he'd been with. She imagined Neil turning around, blushing from the sun and his actions, to search for her, Athena in tow. He would return to the car to find only an empty space. He and Athena would be stuck together – nowhere. And she, Charlotte, would be gone.

The road was narrow and she concentrated on clinging to her side of it, but, when she glanced across, the sky seemed alarmingly within reach. A bus approaching her caused her to almost drive up the rocks, and then a convertible beeped insistently behind her. A man in it stood up to scream at her in Greek. She'd crossed the middle line, forcing them near the edge. It was so treacherous! She steered into a dirt turnoff, grinding the tires against the gravel and turned off the engine and leaned against the wheel.

Neil had once asked, 'Where would you like to travel to, Char? Above all else?' And she'd answered the land of myths and stories, of Zeus, of Sophocles – all those ruins. Neil had brought them to Greece because of her yearnings. She had been longing to sit on stone benches in a Greek theatre, imagining distant masks and grandiose sufferings. She'd wanted to sense the old prophecies, conjure the faith of the ancients, find solace in the temple of Apollo. But now he'd ruined everything. Romance in ruins among the ruins.

Neil had also made a comment about a friend of his. It

was a time when he and Charlotte were particularly close, and Neil told her about an ultimatum his friend had given his wife. 'The guy hadn't been prepared for the consequences,' Neil said. 'He thought he'd get his way. You gotta be prepared to take whatever.' Charlotte stared at the rocks and olive trees, scant at this height. The consequences of her get-even lark could be the absolute end of her and Neil. She'd show him she wouldn't be used or toyed with. But – my god – at a price as steep as this mountain.

She collapsed over the steering wheel. Losing Athens, losing *Neil.*

She thought hard: who was doing what to whom? Had Neil done anything – beyond flirting a bit? Had Athena? She'd made eye contact, it was true, but maybe she didn't know how to play the scene any more than Charlotte did. Why should Charlotte let either of them take away this opportunity to soar on Parnassus? If she had issues with Neil, wouldn't it be better to resolve them where she herself wasn't the primary sacrifice?

She managed to turn the car around in three K-turns, heaving huge intakes of relief along with the dust. She didn't *have to* drive foreign roads for hours. She laughed bitterly. Tolerating Athena seemed simple by contrast.

It took a while to find Neil standing at the high rim of the amphitheatre, his hand shielding his eyes like a surveyor. He waved his arms, signalling where he was. Charlotte had brought cans of orange drink with her, their frostiness keeping her somewhat cool, and offered them as an excuse for her long absence.

'Over an hour?' he said. 'For sodas?'

She studied his face, determining whether he had been worried. She decided he had.

'Libations of "Nitea",' she said, and fought back a thickening in her throat that had suddenly appeared.

He looked puzzled briefly.

'Oh – yeah,' he said.

He took two cans from her and indicated where Athena was, although Charlotte had already spotted the yellow sundress several tiers below. Even from here, she could see Athena clutching a sandal in her hands and rubbing her foot.

'I think she's getting tired of the day,' Neil said. 'This might help.'

Charlotte was still trying to catch her breath with the relief of being back with Neil, of his not knowing about her abortive getaway attempt, as she followed behind him. She sank near Athena on the stone bench and Neil remained standing, surveying what was once the playing arena.

'Charlotte knows lots about all this,' he said, indicating with wide arms the size of Charlotte's knowledge. 'I'm always surprised at what Charlotte knows.'

Charlotte said nothing.

'He is worried,' Athena said. 'Long time we cannot see you.'

'She was getting us these drinks,' Neil said. 'And got lost.'

He was going to pretend to accept the lie, Charlotte realised, the way she'd pretended to accept his contrition over the other woman.

When Neil assumed the driver's seat, he eyed Charlotte only briefly as he re-adjusted its distance from the pedals. Athena insisted on sitting in the back seat. She said all that sun and the lunch had made her sleepy and she'd direct them once in Athens, which she did. They all shook hands and hugged – Charlotte felt stupid here, but went along with

Athena's gesture – when they returned the car.

At the bar in their hotel, Neil and Charlotte ordered gin and tonics. The drinks were warm. No ice, they were told.

'Jesus,' Charlotte said. 'How un-refreshing.'

'It's a constant adjustment here,' Neil said, taking a huge gulp. His eyes met hers for what seemed a long time, as though he would ask a question. Then he did. 'You wouldn't have gone through with it, would you?'

She attempted to wash down the thickness in her throat with warm tonic: *it*.

Neil ordered a second drink, and said, 'What made you change your mind?'

It felt as though they were perched precariously once again, like the experience of physical sensation that lingered long after they'd gone skiing or boating, her body continuing to rock, now with fear.

She shook her head in denial of a reason – or perhaps an inability to frame a reason – tears in her eyes.

'The consequen—' he started, but seemed to think better of it. He asked the bartender for snacks, and said to Charlotte, 'Are we okay now?'

She nodded, embarrassed.

They sat together in silence, having another warm drink, some potato chips, waiting for cues of normality to resume. She pressed her bare arm against his on the bar. 'We are so burned,' she said. He agreed. 'No wonder. All that heat.' He swivelled on his stool and tucked Charlotte's knees between his own. The gesture was a familiar one to her, but her legs felt sticky and she pulled away. 'Even that's too hot,' she said, but then, not knowing what else to do, she kissed him suddenly, briefly. He waited a few seconds and kissed her back. Their mouths tasted of gin and salt and, for the moment, all felt well again.

The following year, Charlotte and Neil went to Norway, where days were cool, and they moved among icebergs with civility. It was the last trip they took together.

11.
Honeymoon with Mata de Limón
Alice Bingner

Stewart Gates, San Diego postman recently retired, picked himself up off the pavement in front of the cathedral in San José, Costa Rica and cussed the driver of the bus which had grazed him as he'd stepped off the curb. He brushed off some of the dirt, examined his body for bruises, found a few, but mostly his dignity had been hurt. His determination had been strengthened.

He approached two or three people walking by, saying 'Train?' as if they'd know he meant to be directed to one. The fourth woman stopped, quizzed '*Señor*?'

He repeated, 'Train?' She caught on, to his relief. She guided him a few yards to the corner, pointed down the hill, held up four fingers, which he assumed meant four blocks, then said, '*A la derecha*', as she gestured to the right. The words meant nothing, but he got the point. He thanked her profusely and hoped that she got his, as he pranced down the hill. He might have been on his old mail route, so happily did he advance. He made the turn correctly because ahead he saw a very old, very dirty, very beautiful building that was obviously a train station.

The din inside would normally have disgusted him, but, with a fervent desire to escape this city he now hated, he got in a line that reached across the entire lobby. He had no idea where he was going. When his turn came, the ticket seller asked, and poor Stew didn't even understand what he'd been asked. Nor did he know the name of a town to go to if he had known. All he really knew was he wanted out of San José at any cost.

A boy of about twelve behind him felt for him in his bewilderment. '*Señor,*' he said, '*Tren a Puntarenas?*'

'*Si, si,*' Stew said, having no idea where Puntarenas might be.

The lad took a dollar from the several that Stew extended and gave it to the cashier to buy him a ticket to the west coast of the country. Had the train waiting on the track been going to Puerto Limón on the east coast, Stew's entire future would have been different. He thanked the boy over and over, offered him the rest of the dollars in his hand, but the boy accepted only the few cents in change. Stew had no idea what any of it was worth. He'd arrived only hours before, in a breathtaking landing between menacing mountains. The natives on board had applauded as the pilot landed safely. Stew had understood their enthusiasm. Out of fear, he hadn't been able to move a muscle until the plane had emptied.

Stew never saw the helpful boy again but, by the time I met Stew three months later and heard the entire tale, the child had become an icon. He was the prologue to Stew's new chapter of life. He symbolised the Ticos and Ticas, whom Stew had come to love like his own kin. Better than his own kin. I don't know how many times I heard the story of his arrival, not in Puntarenas, but in Mata de Limón, fifty miles short of his destination.

It seems he'd been fascinated from the time he'd left the Maidenform Bra billboard, as the train pulled out of San José and passed station after station, where no one seemed to get on or off much, but the mail got dropped and a bag lifted up, the most interesting activity to him, as they picked up speed and, a few miles further on, saw the blink-blink at another stop.

At a larger town, which turned out to be Orotina, the train stopped for a supper break – or what seemed to pass as one. Stew's appetite was ready for the fried chicken, boiled eggs, macadamia nuts, boiled field corn and whatever else a bevy of long-haired, unsmiling, tired-looking ladies who boarded had to offer. He bought some of each vender's wares. He left them the change because he had no idea how to figure colones against dollars. This turned out to be generosity that must have made the women's day, because he got the best of whatever they sold from that day forward, when the train stopped in Orotina.

Just as the train chugged past the cemetery on the way out of town, Stew glanced back and saw the one word he'd be coached on by the stranger in his corner bar at home: *cerveza*. He slapped his hand to his high forehead. He'd passed up a beer – the one thing he needed more than food after his harrowing day. What was he thinking about! A boy had boarded briefly, selling Coke, which he'd bought in desperation, never dreaming that, a block down the track, the nectar of the gods . . .

At any rate, his vigour was renewed with the mixture he'd indulged in and he'd been more alert thereafter. He dozed for a while. A loud call from the conductor woke him. He didn't comprehend a syllable of the announcement. He did, however, glance out the window curiously and see, blessedly, a homemade sign in what turned out to be the Cantina Clara Luz: *cerveza*.

The train had slowed, but not to a standstill. Yet passengers were jumping off with agility. Hell, he could do it if they could. He'd done worse on D-Day. Sure it was a long time back, but, not to be daunted, he tossed his small satchel out the door and swung to the ground, shakily, after it.

He gingerly crossed the tracks and entered the Clara Luz in a spirit of adventure. He dropped his bag on the spotless floor, surveyed the simple room with its half dozen worse-for-wear tables, its chairs that threatened to give way when he plunked his ample body in one. He held up two fingers for the teenage waitress and formed a bottle-tipping gesture with his other hand. Quite bravely, as he described his move later, he uttered his one word of Spanish: '*Cerveza.*'

In a flash, the young girl plopped two opened bottles of beer before him, smiled, made no announcement of cost, and retreated. Stew's brilliant blue eyes followed the Tica in amazement. He'd spoken his first foreign word. She'd understood. She'd welcomed an alien with a smile to a strange land. Stew repeated endlessly, 'I was home. It was love at first sight for Mata de Limón.' That's where – he found out the next day – he had alit from a moving train to find Utopia.

Someone anonymously poured him into a bed in the hotel across the tracks, after he'd held up his two fingers for more *cerveza* heaven knows how many times. He woke to a glistening 6 AM sun in his eyes, only slightly the worse for wear. His duffel bag lay intact beside him. He stood and looked across a wide river. Mud flats, peppered with aggressively hungry gray birds, indicated that the river had been wider recently. In fact, it receded before Stew's very eyes, his second mystery of the morning. He ventured out on a narrow walkway above the river, wisely not leaning against the rail. He looked in the three directions he could see and no road was in sight. 'I knew I was in town,' he told of his introduction to Utopia. 'I remembered the depot. But no roads! Had I died and gone to heaven actually crossed my foggy mind.'

The way he'd heard about Costa Rica in the first place was by telling a man he met in his neighbourhood bar that – in answer to his question – his goal for retirement was to get away from traffic. 'A Ford killed my wife in a collision,' he told the man. 'My daughter was knocked up in the back seat of one, and I haven't seen her since she eloped with the guy. I banned cars from our household but, wouldn't you know it, my two sons found drag racing to be their priority. I can't tell one of them from the other for grease on their faces. I need relief! I hate Henry Ford almost as much as I hate Adolph Hitler.' He bought the guy a beer.

In reply, the fellow gave Stew a welcome tip: 'I just came back from business in a country where some people have never seen a car,' he said. Stew's ears strained for the name of it.

'I'm as good as packed,' Stew said. 'Tell me how I get there.'

'It's Costa Rica. Take a supply of Kennedy half dollars. Oh, yes, and a Polaroid. Those Ticos love to have their picture taken. The only word you need to know as a starter is

'*Cerveza*.' That way, you'll get your beer, and you can point to anything else you want to say in a pocket dictionary. That's what I do. You can take a train from coast to coast. I love it.'

Stew thought it was beer talk, but he couldn't resist investigating. That very night, he packed for a short trip, called for a plane ticket to a country he'd heard about for the first time. Next morning, he bought the Polaroid and a lot of film, and went to the bank. They sold him as many Kennedy half dollars as he felt he could carry. One of his sons' feet were, as usual, sticking out from under a needy junker in the driveway. Stew nudged them as he went by, 'Going on a little trip, son,' he said casually.

'Good for you, Dad. You earned it. The house will be fine with us, so don't worry. Send a card.' He didn't even come out from under the car all the way to make his speech. Stew caught a cab to the airport, clutching the sides all the way. He wasn't kidding. Cars were not for him. He saw trains in his future, even if the stranger's story sounded too good to be true.

'Aggie and I were going to take trains everywhere if she'd lived. I'll have to do it by myself and she'd approve,' he said to himself. 'I raised the three kids and, yes, I've earned it.'

He was amused when he thought of the stranger telling him to expect to find his own holy grail in the adventure ahead.

I found Costa Rica the same year Stew did. In fact, I'd gone to Puntarenas on the train and was venturing back to San José when the train stopped at Mata de Limón. I saw a lake in the background through an arch that spanned a sidewalk toward a hotel, on which I read 'Luna de Miel' which made no sense to me. I wasn't in a hurry. Why not get off and look around? I left my bags in the postage-stamp-sized station, with a kindly attendant, and strolled down the sidewalk to a pavilion that seemed to be the restaurant. I sidled into a chair, timidly.

I was one of two diners. The other one, a man with skinny legs sticking out of cut-off khakis, seemed hidden behind what, unbelievably, looked like the *New York Times*. Two malnourished dogs lapped at crumbs from beneath now-unoccupied tables, as well as the reader's table.

Ducking under the counter at my left darted the plainest young lady I may ever have seen. She approached for my order but stopped abruptly, turned excitedly toward the other table. '*Gringa, gringa*,' she called, pulling at the man's arm. She dashed back to me, '*Gringo, gringo*,' she said, pointing to the now-alert fellow in the Harry Truman shirt.

He rose and moved toward me with blue eyes misting almost to tears. A broad smile exposed a chipped front tooth. His hand extended to me. 'I'm Stew,' he said, 'I haven't spoken English for three months. Let me buy you breakfast and don't expect to get a word in edgewise for the first hour. I can't tell you how I welcome you.' He ordered what seemed to be the only breakfast served: standard and good. Stew began to tell me all that had happened to him since he'd landed in the country, a lot of which I sorted out later.

He was right. I got in no more than the occasional 'Oh no!', and nodded yes or no to indicate I was listening to his life story. I was fascinated by what he was doing in an infinitesimal railroad town in Central America without even a superficial knowledge of the language.

Stew hadn't talked long before I knew he was a man of

intense likes and equally intense hates. Among the former were trains, beer, football, the *New York Times* and Ticas. Among the latter: as a WWII vet, he hated Hitler; as the victim, he felt, of motor vehicles, he hated Henry Ford.

He told me about bringing back his teenage bride from England after the war. They'd had a daughter and two sons before Aggie had been hit and killed by a Ford driver. He had raised the kids alone, banning cars from the household. As was natural, his sixteen-year-old daughter dated in them and his boys took to drag racing like pelicans to fish.

'They'll never give me grandchildren. They're married to Henry's offspring,' he tried to joke. 'I kept my eye on the doughnut since Aggie died and, here I am, a stone's throw from a train and not a car in sight.'

Then he told me about that fateful day in San José, in bumper-to-bumper traffic on streets wide enough for oxcarts. He'd been with the light, he said, 'Imagine? Still I got knocked down.'

I told him about the man I'd met who had explained: 'I've lived in the States, and you have to prove you can't hit a pedestrian before you get a license. Here we have to prove we *can* before we get ours.' His joke didn't sound all that funny to Stew.

He told me about his weekly trip to San José to pick up the *New York Times*, which he'd arranged to have saved for him at a stand. 'I take pictures at the stops,' he said, proudly. 'My artwork graces more mantels between here and San José than the Virgin Mary, I bet.'

Stew got his yen for trains at an early age. 'We were poor. Lived on the wrong side of the tracks, so to speak. For me, it was the right side. I could spell "Chesapeake and Ohio" before I could spell my own name. My mother saved to buy me a Lionel engine when I was six or seven, during the Depression. She added a car whenever she could. She knew how I loved that train that went by, the high point of my day. I joined the army as soon as I could, just to ride a troop train. Now look at the marvellous monster at my doorstep.'

Stew lived in a room of the Manglares Hotel, where we ate. It cost fifty cents a day. Except for the lack of English speakers to share his thoughts with, he said he was in heaven. 'I take the train to San José for my papers and read them one at a time on the correct days. So I'm a week late. I can't do anything about the news anyway, as long as I don't bet on the Dodgers after the game is done and they lost.' He laughed. 'You're the first person I could have bet with anyway. These Ticos spend their days like birds, scratching for enough to live on. They'd have no time to go to a baseball game if there was a team around.'

Breakfast long since eaten, Stew suggested he show me the town: 'It'll take all of five minutes. You saw the depot. There's a *pulpería*. The Clara Luz *cantina*. Not much else. This hotel is the social centre. Careful not to lean on that rail,' he demonstrated. 'It's a killer.'

He pointed to the estuary below, flowing in. The lake I'd seen from the train was not a lake at all. It was the estuary, which, twice a day, with the tide, looked like one and had to be boated across. When the tide was out, you could walk the width of it. In Mata, you didn't tell time by the clock, but by the tide. I saw a house across the way, which Stew said was for sale. 'Why would anyone want to live on that narrow stretch between the Gulf and the estuary?' I asked out of curiosity, never dreaming how it would figure in my future.

'See those kids fishing with a string, winding their lines on Clorox bottles? I buy all they catch every day for a Kennedy half dollar. Ticos dote on that coin ever since Jack Kennedy sent the National Guard to help them when a volcano choked San José with lava during his term. The kids are ecstatic, and I have fresh fish for supper. Anna – you met Anna Delia – the girl at the hotel, cooks them. She's my *novia*. We're getting married on her seventeenth birthday.'

Stew had said something that I couldn't appropriately comment on with an, 'Oh, no!' He could see the expression linger on my lips.

'I know. I know,' he said. 'I'm old. She's young. But Ticas don't care. Boys their age aren't able to offer stability. My pension is like riches in this community. I'm the official loan officer, beer buyer, moneybags. At home, I'd be nobody, eking by. Sometimes people pay me back or buy me a beer, sometimes not. So what? I've found the grail that that stranger said I would. It's a miracle. Cars are out, trains in, and I'll marry another country girl in a year or so.'

Stew did look old beside the teenager, but he felt young. That counted. His enthusiasm for everything was that of a young man.

'How can you plan a wedding when she knows only *gringo* and *gringa* and all you know is *cerveza* and *novia* in Spanish?' I asked.

'Easy,' he said, patting his pocket dictionary. He had a small notebook and pencil at the ready. He showed me the name of their church, the trousseau they bought week by week. 'We've got the ring and other jewellery. She's as happy as a pig in mud and so am I.'

We drank a Coke at the *pulpería*. 'These people put this

crap in baby bottles,' Stew said with disgust. 'They believe the ads that say it's nutritious.'

We strolled over the bridge that crossed the estuary. Missing boards left holes that could have swallowed a baby buggy. Natives of all ages casually walked around them without complaint. A sandy street of huts stretched ahead of us. We turned, though, and went back to the hotel, a sprawling one-story building with its few rooms facing the river that the estuary formed.

A boy of about five saw us return and ran up to Stew, '*Foto, foto!*' he cried, pleadingly. Stew got his Polaroid. He, I found, could not resist a child. As the colours in the picture emerged, the boy's eyes popped. He squealed. '*Gracias, gracias!*' He must not have been introduced to Stew's magic before. He flailed the snapshot with glee as he ran from the restaurant.

Stew said, 'These kids are like the grandchildren I'd love to have.'

As we heard the next train approach, Stew walked to the tiny station with me and we exchanged addresses. We'd write. But I could see why Stew was hooked on the primitive little paradise. It wasn't the last time I'd be there myself.

When I visited Mata de Limón, I brought Stew thick paperbacks to read, and when I was home, he sent me thick accounts of the goings-on in his Eden. Many of them, he wrote from one of his favourite bars: the one beside the cemetery in Orotina, or the one he favoured along a channel in Puntarenas, where he watched the barges go by and the prostitutes ply their trade, and drank his beer and described it all to me.

I noticed that his praises of Anna Delia lost strength as

time went on. The wedding day had approached and been postponed. I said to myself, *This bodes ill.* Anna had acquired some coveted possessions. Stew, not the dirty old man some suspected he was, had preserved her innocence. Successive postponements, he took nonchalantly. She'd brought youth, hope, and excitement to his life, but she'd passed the bewitching age. In spite of his white crew cut, his white beard, his beer-belly bulging over the inevitable cut-offs, his taste in females seemed to be arrested at about age sixteen. He told me once, 'You leave Gringoland and move in with me and you'll never have to worry about a thing as long as I live. Just keep in mind, I don't go for *Norteamericana* women, and none old enough to vote.'

I watched, read and listened to Stew's affections switching from Anna Delia to one sister and then another. In each case, the wedding date came and went; he'd had the attention, they'd had the gifts and a certain prestige. No one seemed disappointed at the outcome.

Remember the house I saw across the estuary the first day I met Stew? The one sitting precariously on a narrow peninsula between the Gulf of Nicoya and the estuary? I had scoffed at anyone wanting to live in such a vulnerable spot, subject to high tides, huge storms, even earthquakes. I bought it. And, yes, I did live through all of the above. I never regretted it.

Stew had always shared his ups and downs with me. One prime 'up' had been his getting acquainted with his English-speaking banker, who was helping him attain *pensionado* status, so that he'd never have to leave his Eden. They met every Monday when Stew took the train to San José to get his newspapers. One particular Monday, Alexis was out of town. Stew picked up his bundle of papers and headed for the pub, planning to read the Monday issue over breakfast and then carry the rest home.

The *New York Times* spread in front of him, he was engrossed enough to be startled to hear in excellent English, 'May I serve you, sir?'

He looked up into big brown eyes, half covered by light brown hair, surrounded by an ivory complexion, a beauty quite unlike the country girls he'd been courting. The waitress, thinking his silent awe was a lack of English, tried her question in French. Still stunned, Stew stuttered an order. He wrote me, 'I don't know *what* I ordered but, as she went to get it, I saw a dream walking.'

Stew ceased writing me after that about nature's marvels on our black-sand beach, about the wide-winged manta rays that heaved themselves out of the Gulf so far away that he'd see them splash before hearing the report of it. About the primitive dogs we both loved, diving into the surf to come out with fish or digging ferociously in the sand to find bright-coloured crabs for their lunches. All he wrote about were Patricia's charms.

Before his last beer that Monday, he'd decided to talk Patricia into becoming his housekeeper. They took a bus to the hovel she shared with a large family, got her mother's consent, packed her few possessions and caught the last train to Mata de Limón.

Meanwhile, I'd bought a ticket to attend his wedding to Vilma, which, not surprisingly, had gone the way of the others at age seventeen.

I read on the way to the airport, 'My new housekeeper can't cook, won't wash or iron, but the local ladies need the work. Patricia pays her way when she walks across the room to make me a mean cup of instant coffee.' *Same plot*, I said to myself, *new leading role*. I was half right.

Stew's letter failed to prepare me for his walking dream. Anna Delia had laughed with him, not at him, as they stomped around the dance floor. Patricia had no such compassion. 'No *thanks*,' she sulked when invited to dance. The country Ticas had made him feel vital, loved his flattering them with newly learned words, like *bonitas muchachas*. Patricia scoffed at his efforts. They exclaimed in awe at his gifts. Patricia never said thanks.

I concluded that Stew had had no real desire to consummate the marriages he had planned. Maybe he doubted his potency. Maybe he aimed for the unattainable for some other reason. He had overwhelming respect for the young girls, and I think he believed they had loved him. As with his train rides to the city, he enjoyed the trip, not the destination.

The village had blossomed in his presence. He gave Christmas parties and engagement parties, the Manglares rang with *marimba* bands and dancing, with *piñatas* and merrymaking at the least excuse for a celebration. No one for miles around was excluded from the Cokes and beer. The good *gringo* became a legend in his own time.

Enter Patricia. A separate entity. *Her* seventeenth birthday obviously would not pass without disappointment if Stew made altar-bound plans that fell through. No matter how she acted, to him she could do no wrong. I believe the love he'd felt for Aggie in London had revisited. He spoke of similarities in their complexions, in the French that Aggie had spoken to soldiers on 'R&R' when he'd met her in 1942, of the fact that they were both waitresses and both the same age.

Even though Patricia clearly played Stew for a sucker, displayed no sense of humour, and showed neither the whimsy he usually enjoyed nor the kindness of the country girls, Stew had fallen so deeply in love this time that he didn't recognise her cunning.

'She's like an idol to me,' he said, almost apologetically.

When I met Stew's banker friend, Alexis, I spoke of my misgivings. He agreed the stage was set for disaster.

Back again in Michigan, I received missives, one of which said he'd proposed to Patricia and been turned down. 'I think, in time, she'll marry me,' he wrote, optimistically. 'You be sure to come so I'll have someone on my side of the church.'

Then along came a thin letter, ominous in that it didn't require Stew's usual double postage. He used no salutation.

'Patricia is pregnant,' assaulted my eyes. My confidence in Stew's impeccable integrity was shaken. I stopped reading for a minute. Then read on.

'NOT ME,' he printed in caps. 'I wish it were. She went down to the beach with a boyfriend I didn't know about.' I'd have suspected he was protecting non-existent innocence in her case. 'I want more than ever to marry her and give the child my name. She says no. More later.'

Every letter following that one updated me on Patricia's condition. She stayed on with him, making the instant coffee and no more. Her salary continued. He pre-paid her hospital bills. 'She might marry me after the birth,' he'd say in most letters.

After the appropriate number of months came the letter about the momentous birth. Stew's enthusiasm emanated from the pages. 'His name is Pablo. We call him Pablito. He is the son, the grandson, the miracle I've always wanted. Patricia still won't marry me, but I won't give up. I must have this boy with me. In a few days of his life, he's become MY life.'

Patricia had a plan of her own.

She lived with Stew off and on. His love, I saw as I read his letters, switched from Patricia to Pablito. She had to have felt it too. She'd whisk the beloved child away intermittently and leave Stew devastated. She'd return; he'd be elated. She'd leave without Pablo. Stew would hire a nursemaid and revel in his new responsibility. He dreaded the day the train bearing Patricia would pull in to the station, a stone's throw from the house he had built after his beach house had been confiscated.

Alexis wrote that Stew drank heavily when Pablo was gone. When the child was with him, he moderated his habits. Stew wrote, 'I even eat vegetables now, so Pablito will too.' He sent scrawls the child would draw of English words Stew had taught him. Alexis wrote that, to see Stew take Pablo across the still-worsening bridge to school, they 'look like a Hummel sculpture'.

Pablo's birthdays required even bigger celebrations at the Manglares. I declined Stew's pleas to come to them. When Pablo was three, Patricia married a *gringo*, according to Stew.

'She's taking Pablo to Pennsylvania. My life is the pits. I want to adopt him. He's a grandson to be proud of . . .' Patricia knew better than to kill the goose that laid the golden egg.

Alexis wrote spasmodically of Stew's extreme grief and his stepped-up consumption of *guaro*. I heard less and less from Stew himself until before Christmas one year.

'Patricia says if I send her two tickets, she'll bring Pablito home for the party this year. I went down on the double and have mailed them to her. Please, please join us. I think she wants to LEAVE Pablito this time. I feel it in my bones, and I couldn't be happier. I knew she'd get tired of him in the marriage to the *gringo*.'

Long distance, I revelled in the carols – Stew sang them in English while everyone else, of course, sang in Spanish – the *piñatas*, the ice cream and cake, all the kids overindulging, the *marimba* band and the beer for the adults, who were also overindulging. But I didn't go down. I didn't want to know first-hand about what I felt sure was to be a major let-down for my friend.

The next thin letter confirmed my suspicion. Pablo had gone back to Pennsylvania with Patricia. She'd had free passage home to see her family. Stew gave up hope. He ended his letter: 'Come on the tenth anniversary of our meeting in this wonderful town and we'll celebrate.' I could feel the village's anticipation.

When I arrived at the hotel and asked, 'Where's Stew?' the clerk wiped her eyes on her apron. She mumbled, 'Cirrhosis of the liver.' I'd come too late.

Alexis arrived later that day. He'd inherited Stew's little house and had come to close it up. He looked less crestfallen than I'd expected, as he too had admired Stew and had become his best friend in Costa Rica. He'd spent a lot of time with him, watching as he brought great pleasure to the humble people who had adopted him as he'd adopted them.

'Stew had been very sick,' Alexis told me. 'Patricia's mother had come to take care of him, but she was at the *cantina* when he died. He was ready to go. I wish you'd been here for the funeral. Stew would have enjoyed it. Imagine: forty kids rode the train to Orotina with him. We buried him in the cemetery next to the bar, the one he missed that first night on his way to Mata de Limón. Men fought for the privilege of carrying his casket. We all managed to take part. It was an unusual sight. Stew would have laughed and stomped his feet for joy at the sight of men, women and children, dressed in their best, some of them riding the train for the first time in their lives, just to be with him on his last day.'

Alexis and I wept as we walked to the depot, passing under the 'Luna de Miel' sign I'd seen the day I met Stew. 'Honeymoon,' Alexis translated. Stew had had a long honeymoon with Mata de Limón. Thank goodness he'd been able to read that 'Cerveza' sign from the train, or he'd have ridden on to Puntarenas and we'd all have missed out on Mata's legendary friend –Pablito's pinch-hitter grandfather.

12.
Refugees of the Meximo Invasion
Gregory Wolos

The tall, pregnant woman with the dark curls spilling around her pie-dish face sat alone in the back row of the chairs arranged for Leonard's Barnes and Noble reading. In front of her, an audience of a dozen tired mothers and wriggling children watched and listened as the author read from *Mend My Tail, Doc*, the latest in his series of Emergency Vet picture books. He'd retired from his veterinary practice and now lived a nomadic life on the road, promoting his stories. Leonard displayed the illustrations: here was the cat being fitted for a prosthetic leg; here the pig with its snout stuck in a peanut-butter jar; here the monkey with its hand super-glued to its tail.

The expecting young woman remained for the question-answer period.

'How long did it take you to make the pictures?' a chubby boy asked around the finger in his mouth.

'I don't do the illustrations. We have an artist for those,' Leonard explained.

'But how long? And what's the matter with your eye?'

'Shh, Jake, be polite,' his mother hushed.

'It's okay, ma'am.' Leonard was wall-eyed. He'd been born with the imperfection his mother had reassured him a thousand times was 'slight'. Frown lines framed her smile whenever she patted his cheek and called him 'my handsome boy'. Leonard's gaze flitted to and from the pregnant woman. She wore a yellow raincoat. 'I keep an eye pointed to the side so I can see if anyone's sneaking up on me,' he told the boy. 'Did you know that a chameleon's eyes work independently? Can you imagine looking at two different things at once?'

The boy blinked, spun his eyes around the room, shook his head and groaned

'Do you have a pet?' a little girl called from her mother's lap.

'Nope,' Leonard said. 'Travelling around to talk about my books, I can't really keep an animal. Sometimes I think a companion for the road would be nice, though.'

'What about children?' It was the pregnant woman. Leonard flinched when she batted her eyes at him: on one of her lids, the left, an extra eye had been tattooed.

'No children, no pets,' he said. 'I'm not married.'

★

The pregnant woman stood nearby as Leonard signed his books for mothers whose children were tugging them toward the exit. Her belly swelled out of her yellow raincoat, stretching her orange maternity shirt as smooth as a pumpkin. She held a large paisley bag by its strap. When he finished, she approached. She was tall – taller than Leonard.

'Your book title's a pun.' Her hands slid over her stomach as if she were polishing it. 'Doesn't docking a tail mean to cut it off? Like for cocker spaniels? So, "doc" is a pun, right? You can't mend something and cut it off at the same time.'

Leonard wagged his head, a nervous habit. He was trying not to stare at her eye tattoo. 'The publisher titled it. But good catch. You're the first to notice.'

'I saw you on *Denver Today* this morning. You told the monkey story. *Loved* it! Would you want to get some coffee? If that doesn't cross some kind of author-fan boundary. Not here, though – somewhere more private. You drive us, and I'll treat. It's hard for me to squeeze behind a steering wheel these days. I'm Mindy.'

She held out her hand, and Leonard shook it. It was dry and cold and strong.

★

When they'd settled into Leonard's Escalade in the mall parking lot, the sun was setting. Mindy rummaged in her bag and pulled out a pistol. She held it by her belly, so it couldn't be seen through the SUV's windows, and angled it at Leonard's face. 'I'm afraid I'm going to have to ask you to give me everything in your pockets,' she said. 'Keep your keys for now. But I want your phone, wallet, everything else.' The gun didn't look like a toy. 'I'm not joking, Doctor Friedman.'

'You're robbing me?'

'No. You won't lose a thing. This isn't a robbery. It's a kidnapping. Or no, a *doc*-napping.' She paused, licking her lips as her attention dipped to her swollen stomach. 'Though I guess it *is* a kidnapping, too. That depends on who you think this baby belongs to.'

Her eyes flashed at Leonard, and she grinned.

'I'm a surrogate mama,' she said. 'Somebody else's zygote has grown to full-term inside me. But I'm calling it mine. I've got a promise of fifty thousand for it in Mexico City. That's double what my contract here calls for.'

She extended a palm toward Leonard.

'So the wallet and the phone–and whatever else you've got that identifies you. Keep the keys in the ignition. Start up and get us out of here – take the interstate south.' Without lowering the pistol she took in the SUV's interior. 'Nice car. How's it on fuel? It's about ten hours to the border and twenty more to Mexico City.'

Leonard couldn't think of the questions he knew he should ask. He tugged his wallet out of his back pocket and his phone out of his front and placed both in Mindy's hand. He started the Escalade.

'So – you want me to be your chauffeur?'

'Oh, you'll be that and maybe much more, doctor. I'm going to call you "Doc", okay? Listen, I could have picked anybody to drive. But I chose you after I saw you on TV and heard you were going to be reading right here in town. What you are is my insurance policy.' She glanced around the parking lot, clutching the gun like it was a small animal needing restraint. 'Just get us out of here. We'll get food and gas on the road. There's a long way to go. I pee often, by the way.'

★

An hour later, Mindy pinned her gun between her knees while she peeled the plastic wrap from the sandwiches she'd bought with Leonard's cash. It was dark. The only light in the SUV was the luminescence of the dashboard and the

194

occasional swimming beams of northbound cars and trucks.

'Do you ever use your four-wheel drive?' she asked, with a full mouth.

'No,' Leonard said. 'I don't even know how it works.'

Mindy swallowed, then rested her sandwich on her belly. 'You got what I meant by "insurance policy", right? You understand your purpose?'

Leonard wished he were taller – long-legged Mindy had pushed her seat back to its limit, and, because his right eye was weak, he had to screw his head like an owl to see her face. He hadn't much of an appetite for his sandwich and chewed mechanically. He'd been thinking about a coincidence: Mindy was a surrogate, and he had once attempted to donate his sperm.

'Is it because being in the car with a celebrity will help if there are border issues?' he asked.

Mindy laughed. 'You're not *that* well-known, Doc. You think customs guys read? I guess they might watch talk shows, though. And they are trained to recognise faces. But, no, don't you get it? You're a *doc*, Doc! I'm due any second – what if my time comes before Mexico City?'

'I'm a veterinarian, not an obstetrician.'

'A baby animal is a baby animal, a delivery's a delivery. I've got towels and alcohol and scissors and a threaded needle in my bag here. I hope we don't need them. There's a clinic waiting for me in Mexico City – if I hold out that long.'

'You could just take some of my money for a plane ticket,' Leonard said.

Mindy patted his shoulder – he felt the thrum of each

long finger. 'That's a nice offer, Doc. Really. But why would I pass up an opportunity to travel with the Emergency Vet? I love your stories! The truth is, I've got passport issues. As in, maybe I've misplaced mine. Or I never got one, I guess. Besides, air travel's unsafe this late in a pregnancy.'

'You'll need a passport to drive into Mexico, or a passport card. I have one in my wallet.'

'We'll cross that bridge when we come to it, so to speak. It's funny – we're sneaking somebody into Mexico when everybody else is sneaking out. But keep both eyes on the road, Doc!'

Leonard had edged onto the shoulder and eased the SUV back into the centre of the lane. 'I've got a problem with my eye,' he murmured.

'Yeah.' She purred a laugh. 'I saw. For a minute there I thought you were getting a little crush on me, sneaking peeks, getting a little Stockholm-ish. You know – Stockholm Syndrome? Everybody falls in love with their captor, right? I've got an eye thing, too – this extra one on my eyelid – I got it when I was fifteen. It's supposed to be spiritual.' She touched Leonard's shoulder again. 'We could get matching eye-patches. Like a couple of pirates. Ouch!' She wrenched herself back in the seat, and her huge stomach rose beside him. The gun was still between her knees. 'Christ, it's hard to get comfortable.' Her pale hands floated like lily pads on her belly as she settled herself.

They drove in silence through the tunnel that the Escalade's headlights cut through the darkness. The tattooed lid made it impossible for him to tell if Mindy slept. An excess of stars swam through the sky – like crystallised sperm, Leonard imagined. Would he share the story of his failure on the long drive to Mexico City? He'd been warned by the clinician: 'Only five percent of potential donors are approved. Frankly, most are college students, much younger than you.' Leonard had continued doggedly through the process – physicals, paperwork, interviews. One night, he had dreamed that he'd been chosen: he'd been ushered into a gleaming white bathroom where, with the aid of *Penthouse* magazine's Miss October – a petite redhead wielding a glass dildo – he'd ejaculated into a plastic cup. Upon exiting, product in hand, he'd been greeted by a crowd of a thousand children, boys and girls who resembled his third-grade photo, the one his mother had framed because his eyes were shut. He'd awoken full of hope, only to receive his blunt rejection in the morning mail.

Mindy's voice startled him. 'This little monkey inside me is a blondie.'

'Excuse me?' Leonard shivered himself alert. He'd need to rest soon.

'This baby I'm carrying – there are rumours about him.' Mindy said. 'I'm not supposed to know who the parents are. Sometimes that's part of the agreement. But I heard nurses talking at the fertility clinic. Sperm from a dead actor, they were saying. I didn't recognise his name, so I googled him. He was old – he died two years ago. But he was blond and very handsome when he was young. I never saw any of his movies. Wikipedia said he was married to a model I never heard of either, much younger than him, also a blond – natural, I think. I read that she had cancer, but recovered. I know chemo makes you sterile, so I figure she had her eggs harvested first, then they cooked up a zygote for the widow with her husband's sperm, and voila!' She patted her stomach. 'But this one's mine now. She's got more frozen zygotes, I'm sure. I wish I could advertise this baby as Hollywood royalty. Can you imagine what he'd be worth?'

Leonard shrugged.

'I saw the way those young mommies were looking at you in the bookstore,' Mindy teased. 'Is that what you're thinking about? Can you tell which moms are single? Or don't you care.'

Leonard face warmed. His head wagged. 'Never—'

Mindy sighed. 'Doc, here's what's going to happen next.' She hoisted herself up as if she were pinned under a boulder and, when he glanced over, he saw that she had again aimed the pistol at his head. She cupped it in both hands as if it were a kitten. 'The next cheap motel we come to, we're going to get a room. Both of us need to sleep. I'm going to handcuff you to the bathroom sink. Underneath. Don't worry, I'll give you a pillow and some blankets. It'll probably be a little uncomfortable – sorry in advance. I'll be stepping around you to pee in the middle of the night. Or maybe I'll need you to deliver the Hollywood royalty. That'd be a riot. Think I can keep the gun on you while that's going on? This is my third pregnancy, you know. First one I gave up for adoption. The second was a surrogacy like this one. But that baby had something wrong with it. They never told me what. I did my part and was paid in full even for a defective—' The sudden illumination of a carcass on the side of the road stopped her short. 'Ugh, what do you think that used to be?'

Leonard blinked at the body as they flashed by – only a long torso, really, its head long gone, its legs crushed to a ruby froth. 'I don't know,' he said. His joints ached. He'd be sleeping on a bathroom floor? But escape was out of the question – he was too weary. 'A coyote, maybe. An antelope?'

'Save *that* one, Emergency Vet.' Mindy yawned. 'Yuch.'

★

The Blue Daisy Motel had one room left with a private bathroom. In it, Mindy offered suggestions for Leonard's comfort: 'You'll have to lie on your back, and we'll cuff your right wrist to the pipe. Wedge your pillow in the corner there. See – you can stretch your legs around the toilet.' The cuffs she pulled from her bag and snapped around his wrist pinched slightly. She grunted as she kneeled to fasten the other end to the drain pipe. 'My stomach's in the way,' she puffed. 'You do it.' After Leonard locked himself up securely, Mindy lurched to her feet. A meaty odour wafted from under her skirt and mingled with the cool air beneath the sink. Leonard stared up at the filthy underside and closed his eyes. How many more bathrooms before Mexico City?

'I'm leaving the light on and the door open. I'll try to tiptoe around you,' Mindy announced. Leonard could only see her legs. Her blue running shoes looked new, and her ankles were swollen and chafed. A quarter-sized bruise yellowed on her shin. The bed springs squeaked under her weight. 'Oh,' she called, 'if you need to go, just give a shout. I'm a pretty heavy sleeper, though. Maybe you'd better hold it.'

★

Leonard woke, stiff, unsure of where he was. His wrist touched something cold and metal, and he jerked it, thinking *gun* – and then he remembered that he was chained up and why. He strained for sounds of Mindy's breathing, but heard only the faucet dripping above him. Mindy liked his stories, she'd said. He imagined that she couldn't sleep and called to him: 'Tell me a story about a time you wanted to save something but couldn't – or you *didn't* want to save something, but had to.' Leonard thought hard. Absent from *Mend My Tail, Doc* were the more lurid stories he'd been saving for an adult version: a frantic, semi-carved steer savaging a slaughterhouse; a manatee with an anchor through its head; a shih-tzu and an eagle locked in a thousand-foot death plunge. Then he remembered a rural emergency from his internship: a distressed cow with Madonna eyes suffering through a breech delivery. The cow stood trembling, and the twig-legs protruding from the leaking opening beneath her tail shook with her.

'Pull!' Leonard's supervisor had shouted, and Leonard had grasped a warm, slick leg and yanked. The calf slid free, and, as he and the newborn slipped to the floor, he'd hugged it to his chest. The smell of blood and raw flesh washed over him. Then his supervisor and the dairy farmer swore at the same time: there was a second calf, a twin, left in the womb. 'Stillborn,' his supervisor had determined with a plumbing arm. The cow and the senior veterinarian struggled to deliver the dead calf while its sibling shivered next to Leonard on the barn's dirt floor, waiting for its mother to lick it to its feet.

★

Mindy's legs! Her greeting dropped from above: 'Morning, Doc. You sleep okay? You were dead out when I came through to pee. Both times. I'm going to wash up, then I'll give you the key so you can free yourself.' She straddled his hips. Water hummed through the pipes and splashed in the sink over Leonard's head. A hand descended with a wet washcloth, and she washed her legs. Her skirt rose and fell with each stroke. He caught a glimpse of her pale underbelly and closed his eyes, opening them when he heard the jingle of the handcuff key.

By the time Leonard released himself, Mindy sat on the edge of the bed, watching him. He craved a long, groaning stretch, but resisted, unwilling to admit his discomfort.

'Hurry up and do what you've got to do,' Mindy said. She clasped her paisley bag under one arm. 'Leave the door open, please. Any funny business and you'll be sorry for it. I'll shut my eyes – that's the best I can do for privacy. What're you staring at?'

The tattoo of the eyeball was missing. There was only a dark smudge on Mindy's lid. 'Your third eye – it's gone.'

She snorted. 'Oh, yeah, that was washable marker. You don't think I'd really tattoo something on my eyelid, do you? Who'd do that to themselves?' She picked up her gun and looked at its muzzle. 'This is all the "third eye" I need, right, Doc?'

Leonard didn't answer. He washed his face and rinsed his mouth, then used the toilet, peeking now and then at Mindy, who, to her word, didn't open her eyes. A smudge instead of a tattoo on her lid was a disappointment – no twin patches; no pirate gang.

★

Back in the Escalade, Leonard behind the wheel, they breakfasted on Twinkies, corn chips and Mountain Dew from the machines in the tiny lobby of the Blue Daisy Motel. The morning sunlight sharpened the borders of the black highway that sliced through parched land. The broken white line leapt at them like machine-gun flak as they made their way south, and the blue sky spread over them as if they were in an enormous tent. Mindy's thumbs fluttered over Leonard's phone.

'I'm going to crack your access code,' she said. She bent over her beach-ball belly, her unwashed curls hiding her face. 'What's your date of birth?'

'Why don't I just tell you the code?'

'No, I want to figure it out. I'm good at it.'

'My birthday's June 28, 1970.'

'6-28-70, no, no,' she grunted as she tested permutations. Leonard peeked at the gun in the folds of her skirt. 'Hey, that's tomorrow! Happy birthday, Doc.'

'Thank you,' he said, surprised. He searched for a birthday memory, but found nothing. Instead, the moment when he realised he'd never marry rose: he'd just finished neutering a ferret and was transferring it to a recovery pen. Its limp body hung from his gloved hands like a necktie. He'd looked at its tiny, shut eyes and thought, 'I will never have a wife.' The words had struck him like a chest punch, and he'd had to sit down, the ferret still dripping from his hands. His failed sperm donation had come soon after.

'I'm in!' Mindy laughed. 'Wow, "628vet". I'll check your messages. Then I'll send some. I'll tell all your contacts that you're on your way to Alaska. Okay, good, the GPS works. I see where we are – and there's Mexico! I love the GPS! It's like a big eye in heaven that's picked us out of nowhere. Mmm, looks like no text or voicemail messages for you, Doc.'

★

'Thank God for air conditioning,' Mindy sighed. Even with open vents blasting at full power, she was flushed and sweating. They weren't far from the Mexican border, according to the last highway signs they'd seen, a fact corroborated by the GPS. The blue had drained from the morning sky, leaving a pale midday haze. Leonard suspected Mindy was planning their assault on the border, and his heart beat faster. She'd been texting busily for an hour – his phone hummed like a jar of bees in her hand. Now and then she mumbled or laughed at something she read without telling him why, and he wished she trusted him enough to share. It had been years since he'd been in the company of another person for so long.

'I have an idea,' Mindy said. 'Let's pretend we're refugees. We're on the run—'

Weren't they? Leonard wondered.

'There's a joke my father used to make. I think it's from my father. I heard it when I was little. Whoever it was said that Mexico and Canada were planning to attack the United States together. There'd be Eskimos attacking from the north, pulled by sled dogs and waving harpoons. Riding up on horseback from the south would be Mexicans with big floppy hats and rifles and those bullet belts crossed on their chests.'

'Bandoliers.'

'Right, okay. They were going to squeeze in on us from the top and bottom. They'd call themselves the "Meximo Army" – Mexicans and Eskimos, get it? You and I are running away from them. We're refugees of the Meximo invasion!'

'We don't use 'Eskimos' anymore,' Leonard said. 'It's "Inuit".'

Mindy hesitated. 'That spoils the joke. It's so easy to ruin a joke. What if,' she began matter-of-factly, 'what if my mother died giving birth to me?' Leonard pictured his own dead mother and the 'handsome boy' lines that marred her smile. He prepared a 'sorry', for Mindy's loss, but hesitated to offer it for a 'what if'. Mindy patted her belly and huffed: 'Woof. Sometimes I forget what I've got going on here. But never for long. If I had no mom, that would explain why I lack a nurturing impulse – no maternal role model. Incubation would be my limit. Would you please pull off here at this exit? Take me off the interstate. I've got to pee before our next move.'

★

Off the highway, they headed due west along a narrow tar road. Weeds grew in its cracks. The dry land, the sparse brush, the gullies and arroyos, the distant hills and cattle fences looked the same as they had from the Interstate, but Leonard felt different, as if the scene had swallowed them, and they were seeing things from the inside. He wondered how difficult it would be to engage the four-wheel drive. The Escalade's owner's manual was in the glove compartment. Would they have to ford a river? Would there be a border patrol that shot first and asked questions later? He sneaked a look at Mindy. She had picked him, something no woman had ever done before. Though they weren't pirates, they shared something. They were pioneers of modern survival. Leonard had been rejected as a sperm donor, but Mindy had given him a new purpose: she was an incubator in need – an *entrepreneurial* incubator – and he was a deliverer.

'Here is good,' Mindy said when the road cut through a sandy stretch along a dry creek bed. Leonard slid the SUV to a stop, the tires crackling and shushing. Mindy still toted the gun, but Leonard doubted she'd force him to follow her while she went off to squat behind a bush or outcrop. She probably wouldn't even ask for the keys. After she did her business, they'd plan the crossing – from north to south, right through the southern outpost of the Meximo Army.

But Mindy didn't budge. 'I think I just saw an animal in distress,' she said, staring straight at Leonard, her face as cold and flat as a china plate. 'I did. Definitely. Down that empty creek bed. It was limping.' Leonard peered past her, to the right and left. There wasn't a sign of movement, and he could see for miles. 'It was a burro, I think,' she added. 'Probably escaped from a ranch. Poor thing. A burro or a mule. What's the difference?'

Leonard focused on the gun, which seemed to have woken up and taken an interest in his chest. Mindy braced it on her belly next to the phone. He choked the wheel. 'A mule is the offspring of a horse and a donkey,' he said. 'Mules are sterile.'

Mindy shook her head. 'I meant what's the difference *what* it is? You've got to investigate, right? You're the Emergency Vet.' She started a deep breath, then cut it short. 'Doc, there's no Mexico City. I couldn't drive that far in my condition. But we're less than an hour from the border now, and my associates are going to meet me when I cross. I'll flash your passport card. Believe me, nobody'll give it a second look. We kind of resemble each other, in a way.'

Leonard's thoughts unspooled – he felt light-headed.

'No contractions yet,' Mindy said. 'I don't need insurance anymore. But it's been nice talking to you. What I would like now is for you to get out and walk down the creek bed – off the road a ways, please. Leave the keys. Just right there in the ignition, thank you. This is a beautiful vehicle. Real value.' Mindy gazed up and down the road. Leonard noticed for the first time that her eyes were the colour of lilacs. 'Let's go, Doc. Think of that suffering creature out there. Who's going to investigate if you don't?' She gestured with the gun. The phone hummed, but she ignored it. 'Go on, open the door and step out.'

Leonard lost his balance as he swung the door open, staggering as he set his shaking legs on the baked ground. Fresh tar oozed from the cracks in the road. The air above it shimmered with heat in both directions. His cheek muscles tightened, and he held his hands out to his sides as if he'd dropped something. His gaze swept across the terrain to the horizon. There was no injured animal.

'Which way did you see it go?' In spite of the dry air, his voice came back to him as if he was underwater.

'It doesn't matter,' Mindy said. 'Just start walking. And don't look back. That way, I guess, off the road. Hurry up.' As he shuffled around the Escalade, Leonard heard the passenger window whine open. He kicked up dust on his way to the creek bed and glared at his feet: his brown moccasins looked new. When had he bought them? Where? He passed rocks and pebbles striped with glitter. When he was a kid, he would have collected stones like them, pretending they'd make him rich. Maybe it had been a hundred years since anyone had looked at these. Maybe they'd never been noticed by a soul.

'Keep going!' Mindy's voice sounded as if she were just a few feet behind him, but he'd walked at least thirty paces. He shivered a breath. His shadow leaned away from him, and he watched it pass over larger rocks and the shrivelled bushes that would become tumbleweeds when they broke off in the wind. A half-hope rose in his throat. Maybe Mindy didn't mean to shoot him. She wouldn't have to– she was going to Mexico. His elbows brushed his hips; he regretted never having learned to walk proudly, and he tried to stand straight. But he didn't want to march. He waited for an instinct to tell him to run. The Escalade started, and the drone of its engine rolled out to him. This would end up no worse than a desertion, he reasoned. He'd need water.

What if Mindy's water broke? What if, as she lowered her smudged lid and tightened her finger on the trigger, she suddenly exploded? The water would gush between her legs and flood the upholstery. Her dress would be soaked. Contractions would begin. Driving would be impossible, and she'd need her insurance policy once again. She'd call Leonard back to the Escalade, but he would plant his feet in the dust, fold his arms over his chest and wait. Until she begged. Time would crawl by. He'd outlast her. Where are your associates now? he might chide. Leonard would have to deliver the baby.

There might be complications. The newborn, a fine boy, would slip into Leonard's steady hands, but Mindy, lying back on the reclined passenger seat of the Escalade, might haemorrhage uncontrollably. He'd drag her bloody and unresponsive body from the car while the infant squalled. Leonard would cover the young woman – she'd either be dead or the next worst thing – with brush and rocks and sand. Then he'd drive south overland while the phone buzzed with orphan messages and all of nature drew toward Mindy's body. Scavengers, sun, and wind would pick her clean until her bones merged with the country.

The boy belonged as much to Leonard as to anyone. Years in the future, Leonard would share with the handsome child the true story of how they came to live in their villa. The Meximo invasion would have dissolved all borders, but Leonard would faithfully describe the world as it had been: he saw himself flipping through a picture book, lingering over each illustration, pointing out details.

But each turn of a page was a scuffed step into the plain, and, as Leonard edged further from the SUV, a question rose like a monument – would he hear the shot before he felt it?